Selma Lagerlöf

Thy Soul Shall Bear Witness

e-artnow 2021

Selma Lagerlöf
Thy Soul Shall Bear Witness

Translator: William Frederick Harvey

e-artnow, 2021
Contact: info@e-artnow.org

ISBN 978-80-273-4020-0

Contents

CHAPTER I
THE STORM WITHIN THE SOUL

It was a poor little Slum-Sister who lay dying. She had contracted consumption of the rapid kind, arid had not been able to resist it beyond a year. For as long as she possibly could she went about performing her usual tasks, but when her strength was quite exhausted she was sent to a sanatorium, where she was nursed for several months without getting any better. When at last the girl understood that her case was hopeless she went home to her mother, who lived in a little house of her own in a suburban street. Now she was confined to her bed in a narrow room-the very same room she had occupied as child and young girl-and was awaiting death.

Her mother sat sorrowful at her bedside, but so anxious was she to bestow ah the care she could on nursing her daughter, that she gave herself no time to weep. A Sister, who had been the sick girl's colleague in the slum work, stood by the foot of the bed weeping silently. Her gaze hung with tenderest love on the face of the dying girl, and when the tears gathered in her eyes she hastily wiped them away. On a small uncomfortable chair, which the invalid so much prized that she had brought it with her when she moved, sat a stoutly built woman, with a big " F " embroidered on the collar of her dress. She had been offered another chair, but she insisted on sitting on the rickety one-as a mark of respect, as. it were, to the sick girl.

It was no ordinary day, this, but New Year's Eve ! The sky without hung grey and heavy, and so long as one sat indoors one fancied that the weather must be rough and chilly, but, once out in the air, one found that it was surprisingly mild and balmy. The ground lay black-without snow; now and again a snowflake fell, but it melted at once. Wind and snow seemed to think it not worth while setting to work to make a pother in the Old Year, but much preferred to husband their strength for the New Year that was fast approaching.

It was much the same with men as with the weather. They, too, seemed unable to set about anything. There was no movement without nor any work-within. Right opposite the house where the woman lay dying was a plot of land where piles were being driven in for a building. A few labourers had come there that morning, had drawn up the great pile-driver, accompanied by the usual noisy song, and had let it drop again. They did not stick long at their work, but soon tired of it, and went their way.

It was just the same with everything else. A few women had hurried by with their baskets to make purchases for the holiday. The traffic had continued for a while, but soon stopped. Children who had been out playing in the street were summoned home to put on their best clothes — and, after that, they had to stay indoors! Carthorses were driven past, to be stabled far away in the suburb, to rest for the next twenty-four hours. The longer the day advanced the quieter everything grew, and the cessation of every sort of noise was felt as a relief.

"It is well that she should die thus, on a holiday," said the mother. "Soon there will be no sounds from without to disturb her."

The sick girl. had been lying unconscious ever since morning, and the three who were gathered round her bed could say anything without her: hearing them. In spite of this, however, it was easy to perceive that she was not lying in a state of dull torpor-her countenance had changed its expression many times in the course of the forenoon. It had looked astonished and anxious; sometimes it had an imploring; at other times a cruelly tortured expression. Now for a long time it had been marked by a violent resentment, that marred and beautified it at the same time.

The little Slum-Sister had become so unlike herself that her companion, who was standing at the foot of the bed, stooped down to the other Salvationist, and whispered:

" Look, Captain, Sister Edith is getting so beautiful; she looks like a queen."

The stoutly-built woman got up from the low chair so as to get a better look at the invalid. Assuredly never before had she seen the little sister without the meek and cheerful mien which she had retained up to the last, however tired and ill she might feel. So surprised was the Captain at the change in the girl's appearance that she did not resume her seat, but remained standing.

By an impatient movement the little Sister had thrown herself so high on the pillow that she was sitting half upright in the bed. An expression of indescribable majesty hovered over her brow, and, though her mouth did not move, she looked as if words of chiding and contempt were issuing from her lips.

The mother looked up: at the two wondering women. "She has been like this on other days as well," she remarked. "Was it not about this time of day that she used to go on her rounds ? "

The Slum-Sister glanced at the patient's battered little watch that ticked on the table by the bedside.

"Yes," she admitted," it was at this time she used to seek the outcasts."

She stopped abruptly and put her handkerchief, to her eyes whenever she tried to say something about the invalid she found it difficult not to burst out weeping.

The mother took one of her daughter's hard little hands into her own, and stroked it.

"She has, I suppose, had far too hard a task in helping them to keep their dens clean, and warning them against their vicious habits," she said, with suppressed resentment in her voice. "When you have a too exacting task, it's hard to keep your thoughts from it. She fancies she is once more on her rounds, visiting them."

"That may sometimes be the case with a work one has loved too much," remarked the Captain quietly.

They noticed how the patient's eyebrows were raised and lowered till the wrinkle between them became deeper and deeper, and how the upper lip curved upwards. They waited, only for the eyes to open and. shoot a glance of withering scorn.

"She looks like an avenging angel!" cried the Salvationist Captain in an excited tone.

"What can they be about in the slums this particular day?" wondered her companion, as she pushed past the others, so that she could stroke the dying girl's forehead. "Sister Edith, don't worry yourself about them any more," she went on, and stroked her once again. "Sister Edith, you have done enough for them."

These words seemed to have power to release the sick girl from the vision that obsessed her; her features lost their look of tension, of majestic wrath. The gentle and suffering expression, which was her usual one since her illness, returned.

She opened her eyes, and, on seeing her companion bending over her, she laid her hand on the latter's arm, and tried to draw, her down to her.

The Sister could hardly guess the meaning of this gentle touch, but she understood the imploring look in the eyes, and bent down to the sick girl's lips.

"David Holm!" whispered the dying girl.

The Sister shook, her head, doubting if she had heard accurately.

The sick girl tried her hardest to make her meaning clear. She uttered the words with a pause between each syllable.

"Send-for-Da-vid-Holm."

She gazed into the Sister's eyes until she was certain that her friend had caught her meaning. This done, she lay down again to rest, and a couple of minutes afterwards she was off again, occupied just as before, mentally present at some hideous scene which filled her soul with wrath and anguish.

The Sister rose from her stooping position. She had ceased weeping, and was seized by a strong emotion that had driven away her tears.

"She wants us to send for David Holm!"

It seemed to be something quite awful that the patient longed for-the big, coarse Salvationist Captain was as much agitated as her companion.

"David Holm!" she repeated. "That's hardly possible, I suppose; nobody would allow David Holm to approach anyone who was dying."

The girl's mother had sat down and seen how her daughter's countenance was working up to that judicial expression of indignation. She now turned to the two embarrassed women for an explanation.

"Sister Edith wants us to send for David Holm," explained the Salvationist Captain, "but we don't know if that is fit and proper."

"David Holm? " asked the girl's mother doubtfully. "Who is he? "

"He is one of those with whom Sister Edith has had a lot of trouble in the slums, but the Lord has not vouchsafed to her to gain any influence over him."

"Perhaps it is God's purpose, Captain," said the Sister hesitatingly, "to work upon him in these her last moments."

The girl's mother looked at her indignantly. "You have had the upper hand with my daughter, you know, as long as she had a spark of-life left. Let me have her to myself now that she is on the point of death."

That settled the matter. The Sister resumed her place at the foot of the bed; the Salvationist sat down on the little chair, shut her eyes, and was quickly absorbed in low murmured prayer. The ' others caught a word or two-she was beseeching God that the young Sister's soul should be suffered to depart in peace from this life, without being troubled and disturbed any more by the duties and cares which belong to this world of trials and tribulations.

Whilst absorbed in prayer she was aroused by the Sister laying a hand on her shoulder. She opened her eyes suddenly.

The sick girl had recovered consciousness once more, but she was not looking so meek and humble as on the last occasion ; something of that threatening storm-cloud still lingered upon her brow.

The Sister stooped over her, and heard clearly enough the reproachful. question:

"Sister Mary, have you sent for David Holm?"

It was likely enough that the others would be prepared to make excuses, but something the woman read in the poor girl's eyes silenced her. "I will fetch him to you, Sister Edith," she promised, and turned apologetically to the mother. " I have never said no to anything Sister Edith has asked me. How can I do so to-day ?"

The girl shut her eyes with a sigh-of relief, and the Sister quitted the little room. "Then all was hushed again. The dying girl's chest laboured more painfully, and. her mother drew nearer to the bed, as though anxious to shield her daughter from death.

A few seconds afterwards the girl looked up. She had the same impatient expression as before, but when she saw that "her companion's seat was empty, she realised that her wish was about to be gratified, and her face assumed a gentler expression. She made no attempt to speak, but, oh the other hand, she did not sink into a coma, but kept awake. An outer door opened, and she sat up in bed. Directly afterwards the Sister looked in at the bedroom door, which she opened as narrowly as possible.

"I dare not come in," she said, " I'm too cold. Captain Andersson, be kind enough to come here for a moment." She noticed at once how expectantly the sick girl's eyes were fixed on her. " I've not been able to find him, yet, Edith," she added, " but I met Gustavsson and two others of ours, and they promised me to have him found. Sister Edith, Gustavsson will be sure to bring him to you if it is at all possible."

She had hardly finished speaking before the dying girl shut her eyes and relapsed into that mood of inward contemplation which had obsessed her all that day.

"She sees him right enough," remarked the Sister. Her voice had in it a ring of indignation, but she corrected herself immediately. "Alleluia ! it's no misfortune that God's will should be done."

She quietly retired into the outer room, followed by the Salvationist Captain.

There stood a woman who could hardly have been more than thirty years old, but who had so grey and almost savagely lined a complexion, such scanty hair and so shrunken a figure, that many an old woman was not so ill-favoured in these respects. Moreover, she was so miserably clad that you might have fancied that she had put on some particularly wretched rags for the purpose of going out begging.

The Salvationist glanced at this woman with a feeling of fast rising anguish. It was not her sorry clothes or her premature old age that was the worst point about her, but the steely rigidity of her features. It was a human being which moved and walked or stood, but who seemed absolutely ignorant as to where she was. She had apparently suffered so dreadfully that her soul had reached a crisis; she might the next moment go raving mad.

"This," explained the Sister, " is David Holm's wife. I found her like this when I reached her house to fetch the man here. He had gone out, and she was pacing there all alone, unable to answer a word to my questions. I dared not leave her' by herself, so I brought her with me here."

"Is this David Holm's wife? exclaimed the Salvationist Captain. "I have certainly seen her before, though I can't identify her. What can have happened to her?"

"It's clear enough what has occurred," replied the Sister sharply, as if seized by an impatient rage; "it's her husband who'is torturing the life out of her."

The Salvationist scrutinised the woman again and again. Her eyes were bulging out of their sockets and their pupils were staring fixedly before her; two of her fingers were incessantly writhing about each other, and time after time a slight shiver ran over her lips.

"What has he done to her?" she wondered.

"I don't know. She could not answer my questions, but sat shivering like this when I came. The children were out, and there was no one to ask. O Lord God, that this should happen on this very day. How can I manage to look after her now, when I want to think of nobody but Sister Edith ? "

"The fellow has been beating her, I suppose."

There must have been something far worse. I've seen plenty of women who have been beaten, but they were, never like this. No, it has been something a great deal worse," the Sister exclaimed, with increasing horror. " We saw, you know, from Sister Edith's face that something terrible had happened."

"Yes," cried the Salvationist Captain ; " now we can understand. what it was that worried her. Thank and praise God that Sister Edith did see, so that you reached there in time, Sister Mary. Thank the Lord and praise Him ! It is certainly His purpose that we should succeed in saving the poor woman's reason."

"But what am I to-do with her ? She follows me when I take her hand, but does not understand a word I say. Her soul has taken flight; how can we recapture it ? I've no influence over her but perhaps you will succeed better, Captain Andersson ?"

The heavily built Salvationist took the poor woman's hand, and spoke to her in a. gentle, but-at the same time stern, voice. Not a glimmer'of understanding, however, was discernible on the woman's countenance.

In the middle of these useless efforts Edith's mother put her head in at the door.

"Edith is getting restless," she warned them; " you had better'come in."

Both the Salvationists hurried into the little bedroom. Edith was tossing backwards and forwards on her bed; but her restlessness seemed rather to have been due to something weighing on. her mind than to actual physical pain. She became quiet directly she saw her two friends in thieir usual places, and shut her eyes.

The Salvationist gave the Sister a sign to remain by the patient, but she herself got up, intending to steal noiselessly out again. At that moment the door opened and David Holm's wife walked in.

She went up to the bed, and stood there with staring, dazed eyes, shivering as before, and twitching her bony fingers till the joints cracked.

It was long before anyone noticed any signs that she was aware of what she saw, but the steeliness of her glance gradually relaxed; she leaned forward, and drew nearer and nearer to the face of the dying girl.

Something defiant and awful passed over the wretched woman ; her fingers clasped and unclasped. The two Salvationists jumped up, in fear that she was about to fling herself on Edith.

The little Slum-Sister opened her eyes, gazed at the dreadful, half-insane creature before her, sat up in bed, and flung her arms around her. She drew the woman towards her with all the strength which she could muster, and kissed her forehead, cheeks, and lips, whispering meanwhile:

"Ah, poor Mrs. Holm ! Poor Mrs. Holm ! "

At first the broken victim of misfortune seemed inclined to draw back, but all at once a shiver passed through her body; she burst into sobs, and fell on her knees beside the bed, her head pressed against Edith's cheek.

"She is weeping, Sister Mary, she is weeping," whispered the Salvationist; " she will not go mad now."

The Sister's hand clutched tightly her teardrenched handkerchief as she mopped her eyes in a desperate effort to steady her voice. " Captain, it's Sister Edith alone who can work such marvels. Oh ! what will become of us when she is gone ? "

The next moment they caught an imploring glance from Edith's mother.

"Yes, certainly," said the Salvationist, with quick understanding; " it would never do for the husband to come and find her here. No, Sister Mary, you must remain with your friend," she went on, when the Sister was about to leave the room. " I will look after this other one."

CHAPTER II
THE BIRTH OF A NEW YEAR

On this same New Year's Eve, but so late that it : was night and quite dark, three fellows were sitting drinking ale and Schnapps in the little shrubbery surrounding the city church. They had thrown themselves down on "a withered grass-plot, beneath some lime-trees, the black branches of which gleamed with moisture. Earlier in the evening they had gathered together in a lap-room, but, after closing time, they sat out-of-doors, as they knew that it was New Year's Eve, and for that reason they had betaken themselves to the shrubbery. They wanted to be near the steeple-clock, so as not to miss hearing when it was time to drink a toast to the New Year.

They were not sitting in darkness, but had abundance of light from the gleams thrown on the shrubbery by the electric lamps in the surrounding streets. Two of them were old and down-at-heel; a couple of unlucky tramps who had slunk into the town to swill up the coppers they had amassed by begging. The third was a man somewhat past thirty. He, like the others, was very shabbily dressed, but he was tall and well built, and seemed to be sound of limb and stalwart.

They were afraid of being discovered and driven off by the police, and that was the reason of their sitting close together, so that they might talk in low tones, almost in whispers. The younger fellow was doing the talking, and the other two were listening with such rapt attention that they let the bottles he for a long while undisturbed.

"Once upon a time I had a chum," said the speaker, and his voice took a serious, almost eerie tone, while a gleam of cunning lit up his eyes, " who was always quite unlike his usual self on New Year's Eve. Not because he had on that day gone through his big account books and was dissatisfied with his year's profits, but simply because he had heard tell of something dangerous and mysterious which might befall anybody on that day. I assure you, friends, that he used to sit silent and anxious from morning to night, and would not once look at a drink. He was not a moody man otherwise, but it would have been as impossible to get him out on a New Year's Eve-for a little spree such as this — as it would be for one of you two to be hail-fellow-well-met with the Lord Lieutenant.

"Ah, well! I suppose you are wondering what he was afraid of. It was something of a job to get that out of him, but on one occasion; however, he told me what it was. Perhaps you Would not care to hear it to-night ? It does feel a bit dismal in a shrubbery like this, which, likely enough, may have been a graveyard in bygone days. What do you think ? "

As the two tramps naturally protested that they did not know what it was to be afraid of ghosts he proceeded to tell the story.

"He had come of a rather superior class, this man I'm telling you about. He had been a student at Upsala University, so he knew a little bit more than fellows like us, you see. And mark you, gentlemen, he kept sober and quiet on New Year's Eve simply so as not to get mixed up in a fight, or expose himself to the risk of any accident, and so come to die on that day. He did not care a rap if he met his death on any other day whatsoever, provided only that nothing fatal befell him on New Year's Eve, for in that case he believed that he would be made to drive the death-cart."

"The death-cart? " repeated his two hearers together, in a tone of interrogation.

The tall fellow amused himself by whetting their curiosity, asking them if they really wanted to hear the story just where they were sitting; but they were eager for him to go on with it.

"Well, this friend of mine," he continued, " always used to assert that there is an old, old cart, of the sort which peasants use for carrying their goods to market, but so dilapidated that it never ought to exhibit itself on the king's highway. It is so bespattered with mud, so dusty and dirty, that one can hardly see what it is made of. Its shafts are flawed, its fellies sit so loosely that they rattle, the wheels have not seen grease within the memory of man, and creak in a way to drive one crazy. Its bottom is rotten, and the driver's cushion is tattered and torn, and half the back of the seat has been broken off. And' this' cart has an old, old horse that is one-eyed, lame, and grey with age in mane and tail. It is so skinny that its spine sticks up like a saw beneath its skin, and all its ribs can be counted. It is stiff-legged, lazy, and ill-disposed, and moves no faster than a young child crawls. For the horse there is harness that is worn out and motheaten, it has lost all its buckles and clasps, and the pieces are joined together with odds and ends of sail twine and birch twigs. It cannot boast a single boss of brass or silver, but only a few sparse tassels of yarn, which are a disfigurement and not an ornament. The reins are in keeping with the harness, for they consist solely of knot upon knot — they have been mended so often that nobody can make any "further use of them."

He got up and screeched out his hand for the bottle, perhaps give his audience time to reflect on that they had heard.

"Perhaps you think this sounds too much like romancing," he said, resuming his story; "but see, the fact is that, besides the harness and the wretched reins, there is a driver, who sits crooked and loathsome on the tattered seat, and drives the old horse. He is blue-black on the lips and grey-blue on the cheeks, and his eyes are as sombre as broken mirrors. He is clad in a long black stained monkish habit, with a cowl which he pulls down over his face, and in his hand he holds a blunt and rusty scythe in a long handle. And, mark you, the man who sits driving, with those reins tied together, is no ordinary driver, but is in the service of a grim master whose name is Death. Night and day he needs must fare on his master's errands. Directly anyone is doomed to die-understand that, friends-it is his duty to be on the spot. He comes rattling along in his creaking old cart, as fast as the lame horse can drag him."

The narrator paused, and tried to get a glimpse of his companions' faces. When he discovered that they were as attentive as he could possibly desire he went on with his story.

"You have possibly seen some picture or other of Death, and you have perhaps noticed that, for the most part, he goes on foot. That is not Death himself, but only his driver. Look you, one might think that, so high and mighty a lord maybe' will garner none but the very finest crops, and will leave to his driver the care of the poor little straws and weeds that grow by the wayside. But now you must pay attention to the most curious thing in this story. Well, the legend is that, though there is always the same cart and the same horse to make the rounds in this particular business, yet it is not always the same driver. That grim figure will be the last man or woman who dies during the year-the one who gives up the ghost just as the clock strikes twelve on New Year's Eve-and is foredoomed to. become Death's driver. His corpse will be buried like all other corpses, but his wraith must don the monk's habit, grasp the scythe, and journey round from one house of death to another for a whole year, till he or she is released on the next New Year's Eve.

He ended his story, and gazed at his undersized companions with a look of crafty expectation. He noticed that they were looking in a fruitless effort to see what time the church clock was pointing to.

"The clock has just struck a quarter to twelve," he informed them, "so you need not have the slightest doubt that the fateful hour has come. Now perhaps you understand what it was that my friend dreaded-nothing except that he might die just when the clock struck twelve on New Year's Eve, and that he might be compelled to become the ghastly driver I have told you about. All that day, I believe, he used to sit and imagine that he could hear, the death-cart creaking and rattling. And, mark you, gentlemen, the curious part of it is that he is said to have died last year on that very same New Year's Eve."

"Did he die immediately before the New Year was ushered in ? "

"All I know is that he died on New Year's Eve, but I've never found out the exact time. Well, well, I might have predicted that he would die at that very hour, because he sat worrying himself about it. If you two got that idea into your heads, likely enough the same fate would overtake you."

The two puny fellows, as if by mutual agreement, each clutched the neck of a bottle and took a long pull, after which they began slowly and awkwardly to stagger to their feet.

"But, friends, surely you would never dream of going your ways before the stroke, of midnight?" cried the narrator, when he saw that he had succeeded all too well in frightening them. "

I can never really believe that you attach the least importance to such an old wife's story as.this. Bear in mind that my friend was rather a weakling-not like us, of good, sound old Swedish stock. Come now, will you take a drink and sit down again ? It will, I think, be just as we'll," he went on, when he had got them down on the grass, " for us to keep our seats. This is the first place where I've had a rest since morning. Everywhere else I was attacked by the Salvation Army people, who want me to go to Sister Edith, who, "so they say, is dying. But I made excuses. Nobody for choice would let himself in for such a beastly sermonising as I should get."

The two tramps, their brains clouded by their last heavy pull at the Schnapps bottle, both bounced up at hearing Sister Edith's name mentioned, and asked if she was the one who was managing the Slum Rescue in that town.

"Yes, right enough, she's the one! replied the younger man. "She has been honouring me with her special attentions all this year. I hope she isn't one of your intimate acquaintances, in which case your grief would be terrible." It was not unlikely that the two tramps retained , some "recollection of a kindness Sister Edith had shown them. " They asserted with dogged determination that, according to their view of the matter, if Sister Edith wanted to meet somebody, no matter who he or she might be, it was that person's plain duty to go to her at once.

"Ha! that's your opinion, is it ? " said their companion. " Well, I will go, if you, whose acquaintance with me is somewhat slight, can tell me what pleasure it would give Sister Edith to meet me."

Neither of the two vagabonds condescended to answer" his question; all they did was to insist on his taking himself off, and, when he repeatedly refused to do so and got irritated with them, they flew into such a violent rage as to declare that, if he would not go of his own accord, they would give him a sound thrashing. Thereupon they got on their feet and rolled up their coat-sleeves to attack him.

Their adversary, who was quite aware that he was the biggest and strongest man in the whole town, was moved with a sudden sympathy for the wretched weaklings.

"If you must needs have it that way," he cried. "of course I am ready whenever you please; but I venture to say that I think, gentlemen, that we might as well make up this quarrel, especially if you bear in mind what I have just told you."

The tipsy fellows hardly knew what had upset their tempers, but their lust for battle was whetted, and they hurled themselves on their companion with clenched fists. So confident-was he of his superiority that he did not trouble to stand up, but remained sitting on the ground. He merely stretched out his arms and warded off his adversaries right and left; as if they had been a pair of puppies. But, like puppies, they returned to the attack, and one of them managed to deal the big man a doughty blow on the chest. The moment afterwards the latter felt something hot rising.in his throat and filling his mouth. As he was aware that one of his lungs was gone, he suspected this to be the starting of a hemorrhage. He stopped fighting and threw himself on the ground, a stream of blood gushed over his lips.

This was of itself a grave misfortune, but what rendered it almost irretrievable was that his companions, when they felt the warm blood spraying over their hands and saw him sinking down, on the ground, believed that they had murdered him, and took to flight. He was left deserted! The hemorrhage, it is true, gradually ceased, but directly he made the slightest effort to rise the blood welled forth again.

It was not a particularly cold night, but the dampness and chill began to torture him as he lay prostrate on the ground. He had a feeling that he was likely to perish unless someone came to his rescue and took him to a place of shelter. To all intents and purposes he was lying in the very heart of the town, and, as it was New Year's Eve, there were multitudes of people up, and he could hear them walking about the streets that ran round the shrubbery-but not a soul entered it. He could even hear the murmur of their voices! It was hard, he thought, that he should perish for lack of help, when help was so near at hand.

He lay waiting for a while, but the cold tortured him worse and worse, and, when he realised that it was impossible for him to^get on his feet, be determined at any rate, to shout for assistance.

Just as he was uttering his cry for help the clock in the tower above him began striking!

The human voice was so completely stifled in that loud metallic clang that nobody noticed his cry of distress. The hemorrhage started afresh, and it was now so extremely violent that he could hardly help thinking that all the'blood in bis body was about to leave it-if it had not, as it seemed, already done so.

"It can't really be possible, that I am to die now, while the clock is actually striking midnight!" he thought, but he had a feeling that he was going out like a burnt-out candle.

He sank down into darkness, and unconsciousness at the very moment that the last booming stroke of the clock died away-heralding the birth of the New Year.

CHAPTER III

THE DEATH-CART

Directly after the clock in the church tower had boomed out. twelve far-resounding strokes, a short, sharp, creaking noise cleaved the air.

It recurred incessantly, at only momentary intervals, exactly as if it arose from some ungreased cart-wheel, but it was a much sharper and more disagreeable sound than that which would come from the most utterly worn-out vehicle. It had anguish in its train it aroused a dread of all the torture and suffering, imaginable.

Lucky it was that this weird sound seemed inaudible to most of those who were waiting to see the Old Year out. If it had been audible, all the merry young people who wandered all night up and down the streets round the. market-place and church shrubbery, and who were now shouting to each other "A happy New Year," would have exchanged their festive greetings for lamentations over all the evil that impended for themselves and their friends.

Had it been audible, the congregation which was ' keeping watch-night in the mission chapel, and had just struck up the New Year's psalm of praise and gratitude to God, would have fancied that they heard mocking howls and yells from fallen spirits, intermingled with the singing. "

Had it been audible, the orator at a merry party, who was standing, a bumper of champagne in his hand, and was shouting for cheers for the New Year, would have stopped his speech to listen to the horrid raven-croak, with its foreboding of failure in all for which he had hoped and longed.

Had it been audible, all those who were watching that night in their silent homes, and ex-amining in the light of their consciences all their actions in the bygone year, would have felt a keen despair at their own helplessness and weakness lacerating, their hearts.

It was lucky that the creaking was audible only to a single individual, and that this individual was one whom it behaved to be brought to disquiet, to the pangs of conscience, and, if it were possible, to self-contempt.

The man who had lost so much blood lay struggling to recover his senses. He thought that there was something awakening him; that a bird with a piercing shriek, or whatever it might have been, was flying.over his head. He had, however, fallen into a delicious slumber, and could not rouse himself from it.

Immediately afterwards he was convinced that the shrieking came from no bird-it was the old death-cart, about which he had been talking to the two vagabonds that was driving through the shrubbery, creaking and squeaking so horribly that he was unable to sleep.

But, half-conscious as he was, lying there, he dismissed from his mind the idea that it could be the death-cart. It was simply because, but a little time back, he had had it in his thoughts that he fancied he was hearing it now. He fell again into a trance-but once more that persistent creaking came nearer and nearer through the air, and would not suffer him to get any rest. At last he began to realise that, what he heard was the creaking of a real carriage; it was no hallucination, but an actual reality, and it gave no hope of any cessation.

Then he realised that he must make up his mind to wake; there was no other course open to him.

At once he observed'that he was lying on the same, spot, and that nobody had come to his assistance. All seemed just as it had been, but a couple of short and sharp creakings passed through the air. They seemed to come from a long distance', but they, were so persistent and ear-piercing that he immediately made up his mind that these were the sounds that had awakened him.

He wondered if he had been lying unconscious for any length of time-but that did not' seem probable. There were people so near that he had heard them, just recently, shouting to each other "A happy New Year." From this he concluded that it could not be much past midnight.

The creaking recurred again and again, and, as the fellow had always been sensitive to strident sounds, he decided that it would be as well if he ventured to get up and go his way, so as to escape the noise-anyhow, he would make the attempt! He felt in excellent health after waking up. It, no longer seemed as if he had an open gaping wound in his chest; he was no longer chilly or tired, and did not feel conscious of his body, as is usually the case when a person is in perfect health.

He was still lying on his side, just as he had thrown himself down when the hemorrhage had started, and now, in the first place, he decided to turn himself on his back to test what his far from robust body would stand.

"Now I am going to lift myself on my elbowvery, very carefully," he thought; "then I'will turn round and let myself down again."

The man was accustomed-as we all are-when his mind said : " Now I'll do this or that," to find the thing done instantly, but this time it happened, strangely enough, that his body remained lifeless, . refusing to carry out the prescribed movement. It simply lay completely inert!

Was it possible that he had lain there so long that, he had turned to ice ? But if he were actually frozen, then he must be dead-yet obviously he was alive, for he both saw and heard. Besides, it was not cold ; moisture was dripping-dropping from the trees above him.

He had been-so busy wondering what sort of paralysis had seized him that he forgot, for a moment, that excruciating creaking. But now he heard it again.

" Yes, David," he thought, " there is no possibility now of escaping that music; you must put up with it as best you can."

It was not easy for a man who, a moment before, had felt well and hearty, and was not in the least ill either, to be patient when lying inert. He made incessant efforts' to move at any rate a finger, or raise an eyelid, but everything was equally impossible! He began to wonder how he acted in former days when he could move. He fancied that, somehow or other, he had forgotten the trick!

Meanwhile the creaking kept coming nearer and nearer. It was not far off now, for he could hear that it proceeded from a vehicle which was coming very slowly down Long Street in the direction of the market-place. It must be some wretched shandrydan that was coming, no doubt about that. Now he could hear not only how its wheels were creaking, but also how the wood-work was rattling, and the horse slipping upon the wood pavement. It could not sound worse if the wretched death-cart —for which his old friend had such respect-were approaching.

"We two, David," he thought, "are not as a rule particularly partial to the police, but if they were to turn up now and put a stop to this awful row, we should be-grateful to them."

The man had always bragged about his strength of mind, but now he began to fear that this creaking music, combined with everything else that had happened to him that night, would put a stop to that. He had some disagreeable apprehension of being found lying there, and, on the supposition that he was dead, being put into a shroud and buried.

"You will have to he and hear all that is said around your dead body-and that is unlikely to sound much prettier than what you are listening now.".

Probably it was the creaking that made him, for once, think of Sister Edith-not, however, with any sort of remorse, but with an angry feeling that she had, in some way, got the better of him.

The creaking filled the air and pierced his ears, but it failed to arouse in the man any repentance for the wrongs he had inflicted on others, but only angry recollections of all the- disagreeable and evil things that others had inflicted on him.

Whilst he was most bitterly bemoaning his lot, he paused and listened intently for a whole minute. Yes, true as he was alive, the vehicle had passed through Long Street, but had not turned off towards the market-place; the horse was not stumbling any more upon the little round paving stones-it was tramping on a gravel path-it was coming in shrubbery

In his joy at the thought that he could possibly get help, the man tried hard to stand up,, but that' effort was as ineffectual as the previous one. With him it was only thought that seemed capable of movement. But to make up for that he heard the old cart coming nearer, and all the time its woodwork was groaning, its harness was grating, and the unlubricated wheels were painfully creaking. It sounded so utterly decrepit that he began to fear that it would tumble to pieces before it reached the spot where he lay.

It moved so incredibly slowly, too> and, impatient1 as he had been at lying helpless and alone, he fancied that it-was taking more time to reach his spot than it actually did. What sort of a vehicle . it could be that was making for a shrubbery in the dead of New Year's night was a puzzle to him. Perhaps the driver was drunk, otherwise he would not be taking such a course. No help could be got from him if that were the case !

"It's the creaking that is making you so despondent, David " he said to himself " The cart has not turned down another alley, as you are imagining, but is making straight for you."

The thing could not be more than a few steps from'him now, but it was the dreadful creaking which he could not stand, that had cooled his courage.

"You are out of luck to-night, David," he continued. "' You will find that it is a fresh bit of illluck that is coming to you. Some heavy roller is going to run over you-or something cheerful of that sort!"

The next moment the man saw the thing that he had been waiting for-though it was not a roller coming to crush him it was frightening him out of his wits.

As he could not move his eyes any more than any limb of his body, he could see only what was right in front of him. As the creaking vehicle came from the side, it appeared in parts. The first object to display itself to him was an old horse's head, with a hoary foretop and blind in the eye which was turned towards him. Next came the fore-part of a horse, which had only one short stump left of one foot, and carried harness mended with bits of string and birch twigs, and adorned with-dirty tufts of yarn.

Such was the sight presented by the whole of the hoist, the whole of the wretched cart, with the back of its seat broken, and loose wobbling wheels —a common market-cart, but so badly used by age that no wares, it seemed, could be carried in it.

The driver occupied his seat, and his appearance tallied accurately with the description the man himself had but a short time back, given of him and his vehicle. He held in his hands a pair of reins which consisted of a succession of knots, his cowl was drawn over his eyes, and he sat askew, as though bowed down by a weariness that no amount of rest could ever cure!

The man had fainted after his second loss of blood, and thought that his soul had fluttered away from him like an extinguished flame. It was not so now-yet he thought that it was shaken and whirled and agitated in such a manner that it could never come right again. From all that had happened to him before the cart came he ought to have expected to see something supernatural, but, even if he had for a moment entertained some thought or other of the kind, he had attached no importance to it. Now he beheld with his own eyes the apparition such as he had heard described in the legend.

"David, this is going to send you crazy," he thought in his bewilderment. "It is not enough that my body is destroyed; now my mind is going."

What scared him at that moment was his catching sight of the driver's face. The horse had halted right in front of him, and at the same time the driver had pulled himself together, as if he had awakened from a dream. He had thrown back his cowl with a weary movement, and was gazing in all directions, as if looking for something.

Immediately the man on the ground met his eyes he recognised him as an old acquaintance.

"Why, that's George," he said to himself " Though he is strangely attired, I recognise him —I recognise him!"

"Can you tell me, David, where he can have been all this time?" he continued, talking to himself. "I don't believe we have met for a whole year. But George is a free man-not tied with a wife and children like you, David. He must have been on a long tour-come perhaps from the North Bole. I think he does look pale and starved with cold."

He looked very closely at the driver, for there was something strange to him in the expression of the latter's face. Yet it must be George, his old chum and boon-companion! It could not be anyone else. He recognised him by bis big head and hawk-nose, his huge black mustaches and his imperial. This main, who had the look about him which any sergeant-nay! one might say any general-might be proud of, could hardly expect to be recognised by an old friend.

"What are you saying, David ? "The mart resumed his curious questioning of himself. "Haven't you heard people say that .George died last year in a Stockholm hospital, and, precisely on New Year's Eve? I heard-it myself/but this is the first time we two have failed to recognise each other-for this is George to the very life. Just look at him now; as he is getting up. Can it be anybody but George himself, "with that delicate body all out of proportion with his corporal's head ? Eh! what are you saying, David? Didn't you see, when he jumped out of the cart, that he had on a cloak that it looked as if he :was still wearing the long coat, full of holes, that used always to hang down to his heels? Buttoned right up to his neck, now as always, David, and the big red neckerchief that fluttered about his throat j but not a trace of waistcoat or shirt. Yes! just the same George now as in the old days." " The paralytic felt quite cheered up. He would have burst but laughing if, taking it aft together, it had been possible for him to laugh.

"Some day, if we get strong and well again — you and I, David-we'll pay him back for this practical joke of this. He nearly drove me crazy with his queer rig-out, just as if he had laid dynamite under it. No other fellow than George would have dreamt of picking up such a sorry horse and cart, and come driving in them to church ! Never once, David, have you had the chance of getting up such a big bit of foolery as this. George was always a cleverer chap than you."

The driver walked up to the prostrate man and eyed him intently; his countenance was stern and grave, and evidently he did not know the man before him.

"There are two things I cannot make out in all this," thought the fellow: "One is how he found out that I and my pals were sitting on the turf here and so got the idea of coming here and giving us a scare; the other is his venturing to dress himself up just like that Death's driver whom he was always so frightened of."

The driver stooped over him with the same weird look. " He won't be very cheerful, poor "wretch, when he finds out that he must release me," the man heard him muttering to himself.

Leaning upon the scythe, the driver brought his face nearer and nearer; next moment he recognised his friend. Hc bcnt: down towards him, threw back his cowl abruptly, and looked him in the eyes.

"Oh! "he shrieked out," it is David Holm who is lying here ! He was the only one I hoped would be spared from this.

"Ah, David, it is you, it is you!" he cried, flinging down his scythe, and kneeling before bis friend. " All the past year," he went on, with intense fervour and distress, " I longed for an opportunity to say but a single word to you-before it was loo late. Once I was almost able to do that, but, you withstood me, so I could not reach you. I thought I should have the chance one short hour afterwards, because I am now to be discharged from my duties, but you are already stricken down here. Now it is too late to warn you to take heed of yourself."

David Holm listened with tremendous bewilderment.

"What does he mean?" he wondered. "He is talking just as if he were dead. And when was it he was near me and I opposed him ? But, of course," he soothed himself by saying, " he must, you know, play up to the part he is acting."

"I know, David," began the driver again, in a voice trembling with emotion, " that it is my fault that you have come to such a pass as this. If you had not had the ill-luck to meet me you would have continued leading a quiet, honest life. You and your wife would have worked on, and in time reached prosperity. You were young and clever, both of you, and nothing should have prevented you. Be sure of this, David; not a day has passed, this livelong year, without my calling to mind in bitter grief that it was I who lured' you from your industrious habits and taught you my own bad ones. Alas," he continued, passing his hand over his friend's face, "Iam afraid you have gone farther astray than I was aware of, for how else could these dreadful marks have been carven round your eyes and mouth? "

David Holm's good humour began to give way to impatience. " Let there be a stop to this foolery, George," he muttered. " Now, do go and find someone who can help you lift me into your cart, and drive me to the hospital as fast as you can."

"David, cannot you understand what has been my occupation during the last year? " cried the driver. " Do you not realise what kind of cart and horse have conveyed me here ? Do I need to tell you who, after myself, will have to grasp the scythe and hold the reins ? But, David, bear in mind that it is not I who have condemned you to this fate. During the whole of this awful year that is before you, don't think for a moment that I was a free party, and could, therefore, have avoided meeting you to-night. Be well assured that I would have done my utmost, had it been possible, to prevent you undergoing' the same penalty as I."

"Poor Georga must have gone mad," David Holm decided, " else he would understand that it is-a question of life or death for me, and that it will not do to dawdle in this' way."

Whilst these thoughts were passing through his brain, the driver gazed on him with unutterable sadness.

"You need not worry yourself, David, at not being taken to. a hospital. When I come to a sick person, it is then too late to send for any other doctor."

" It's my firm belief that all the witches and evils are abroad to-night and have got up a performance among them," thought Holm. "When at last a fellow comes to me, who really could help me, he is either mad or malevolent, if he does not care a straw if I perish."

"I should like to remind you, David, of an incident that happened to you last summer," remarked the driver. " It was one Sunday afternoon, and you were trudging along the high-road through a deep valley; wherever you looked lay broad fields and beautiful estates with verdant gardens. It was one of those sweltering hot afternoons which sometimes occur in midsummer, and I think you noticed, in the course of your walk, that you were the only one astir in all that countryside. The cows were standing still in the pastures, riot venturing beyond the shelter of the trees, and every human being had disappeared. They must have, betaken themselves to their homes to avoid the heat. Is it not true, David, that this was do?"

"It may have happened, you know," admitted the man, " but I've been out and about so many times in the heat and cold that I can't remember them all."

"Just when the silence was most intense, you heard a creaking behind you on the road. You turned your head and fancied that someone was coming after you, but you could not discover anyone. You looked about you several times, thinking that it was the weirdest experience you had ever had. You heard the creaking quite distinctly-but where could it come from ? It was broad daylight open country, and the silence that reigned was such that nothing else could confuse the sound. You could not realise that it was possible for you distinctly to hear the creaking of a wheel without seeing any cart or carriage. You refused, however, to admit that there might be something supernatural in the incident. If only your thoughts had run in that direction, I might then have made myself visible to you-before it was too late."

David Holm now remembered all about the incident quite distinctly. He recollected that he had peeped behind the fences, and had peered down into the ditches, to find out what it was pursuing him. At last he had become half scared, and had gone into a farmhouse to escape from the pursuing noise. When he had come out again, all had been hushed.

"That was the only time I saw you in the course of the year," continued the driver. " I did all I could to get you to see me, but it did not lie in my power to come nearer to you than was necessary for you to hear the creaking. You were walking like a blind man beside me."

"It is true that I heard the creaking," thought David Holm, " but what does he want me to understand by that? Would he have me believe that it was he who was driving after me on the road ? I may have told the story to someone, but why should he tell it in turn to George ? "

The driver bent over him and spoke in the tone of one rebuking a sick child.

"It is no use your struggling, David. It is not desirable that you should understand what has happened to you. But you know more than well that I, who am addressing you, am no living man. You have heard before this of my death, but you refuse to acknowledge it. Even if you had not heard of it, you have, you know, seen me driving in that fateful cart. In that cart, David, no living man is ever carried!"

He pointed to the wretched vehicle, standing in the middle of the avenue.

"Just look at the cart, and look also at the trees, standing beyond it."

David Holm obeyed his exhortation, and now, for the first time, was forced to admit that he was in the presence of. something which he could not explain. He could actually see the trees, on the other side of the avenue, right through the old cart!

"You have heard my voice many times," remarked the driver, " It cannot be possible that you fail to notice that I speak differently than I did."

David Holm had to agree to that. George had always had a beautiful voice, and so, also, had this driver but it was quite another sort of voice: It sounded thin and high-pitched, and not very audible. It was the same performer, without doubt, but'he was playing on another instrument.

The driver stretched out his hand, and David saw that a drop of water, from the dripping branches above, fell upon it-but the drop was not arrested, but fell clean through the hand to the ground.

On the gravel-walk in front of them lay a fallen bough. The driver took his scythe, thrust it under the bough, and lifted it up again through it-but the bough did not fall cleft in twain; it remained as intact as before.

"Try not to misconstrue this, David," said the driver, "but rather to understand it. You see me, and you think that I am like my old self-but this body of mine is such that those only who are dying or dead can see me. You, therefore, are not to think of my body as anything. It is a home for a soul-just as is your own body, and the bodies of other human beings. You must not regard it as something solid or heavy, or endowed with strength, but you are to regard it as an image that you have, seen in a mirror, and then try to fancy that it has stepped out of the mirror and can speak and move."

David Holm no longer cherished any thoughts of rebellion. He looked the facts straight in the face, and was no longer at pains to evade them. It was, indeed, a dead man's wraith that was talking to him and his own body was that of a dead man. At the same time, however, while admitting this, he perceived that something within him was beginning to work itself up into a dreadful rage.

"I will not be dead," he told himself fiercely. " I will not be a mere phantom and a nothing! I will have a fist that I can fight with and a mouth that I can eat with."

At these words, the rage within him gathered into a dense black cloud which rolled to and fro, sultry and loathsome, and tortured no one but himself, nor that for long, but was ready to burst at the first opportunity.

"There is something which I wish to ask you about, David, because you and I were good friends in old days," continued the driver. " You know as well as I do that there comes a time to every man when his body is destroyed, or so worn out that the soul that dwelt therein is forced to quit it. The soul, however, trembles and shivers in. anguish at entering an unknown country. It stands much in the same way as a child by the seashore, that shrinks at committing itself to the waves. Before it dares to take the plunge, it must first hear a voice from someone, already in the Infinite, so it may understand that no peril awaits-then it takes the plunge.

"I have been a voice like that, David, for the whole past year, and such a voice must you be in the year at hand. And there is one thing I will beg of you-do not rebel against this your lot, but accept it submissively ; otherwise you will bring great suffering upon yourself, and upon me."

After saying this, the driver bent his head to look into David Holm's eyes. It seemed almost as if he shuddered at the defiance and rebellion that met his gaze.

"You must remember, David," he persisted, with even more insistent persuasiveness than before, " that this is not a thing you can escape from. I have as yet. not much knowledge of how matters stand on the other side. I have only been taken to its borders, so to speak, but, so far as I have seen, no pity, no mercy, is to be looked for-you have to fulfill whatever is ordained, with good grace or with ill."

Again he gazed into David Holm's eyes, but nothing met him there but the great blackness of a cloud charged with wrath.

"I do not deny, David," he exclaimed, " that to sit in yonder cart and drive-that horse from house to house is the most awesome occupation that could be assigned to any man.- Wherever that driver comes, tears and lamentations await him ! What he has continually to see is sickness and destruction, wounds, blood, and horror. And that is perhaps the least' terrible part of it all. It is far worse to see that which lies within that which is in agony, remorse, and dread of what may come. I have told you that the driver stands only at the threshold —he thinks, as men do, that he sees only acts of injustice, disappointment, unfairness of treatment, fruitless strivings, and confusion. He cannot peer so far into the other world as to discern if there is a meaning and a providence. He can see a glimpse of it sometimes, but, for the most part, he has to fight his way through darkness and doubt. And think of this, David; though it is only for a year that the driver is doomed to drive the death-cart, yet time is not reckoned there according to earthly hours and minutes-as the driver is forced to reach every spot which he is ordered to visit, time for him is stretched out to such an extent that the single year is like thousands of your human years. Although the unfortunate driver knows that he is doing only what he is bidden to do, it is impossible to describe the loathing and disgust he feels for himself, and how he looks upon himself as damned by reason of his office. But worst, of all, David, is that, in the course of his journeys, the driver . also meets the consequences of such evil as he has committed during his earthly life-for how should this be avoided!"

The driver's voice nearly rose to a shriek, and he wrung his hands in anguish ; but he noticed that only withering scorn was gleaming on him from his old friend's eyes. He drew his cowl on, as if he felt chill.

"But, David," he continued insistently, " I say to you that, however hard that which awaits you may be, you must not rebel against it-unless indeed you wish to make it worse for you and for me than it is already. For I must not leave you to yourself; it is my duty to teach you your work, and that, I fear, will be the hardest task ever imposed on me. You can keep me here, with my scythe, for weeks and months-nay! even till next New Year's Eve. My year has expired, but I shall not get my freedom till I have taught you how to fulfill your Office with good grace."

All the time he was speaking, the driver remained on his knees before David Holm, and his words gained strength by the sincere affection with which he uttered them. Still on his knees, he paused for a moment, searching for a sign that his words had produced, some effect; but in his former friend there remained a fixed determination to withstand him to the uttermost.

"It may be that I am dead," thought the latter; " I can't help it if I am ; but nothing shall compel me to have anything to do with the death-cart and the death-horse. They must devise some other work for me —I won't have anything to do with that job." The driver was about to rise from his knees when he suddenly, thought of something that he ought to add.

"Bear in mind, David, that, up to now, it was George who was addressing you; but now you have Death's driver to deal with. You remember, I suppose, whom people have in mind when they talk of him whose decrees are absolute."

The next moment he stood up, scythe in hand, his cowl pulled over his forehead.

"Come out, you prisoner from your prison! " he shouted in a loud and ringing voice.

Instantly David Holm rose from the ground. He did not know how it had happened, but suddenly he was standing upright! He tottered, as everything seemed whirling about him, both the trees and the church wall-but he soon gained his equilibrium.

"Look round, David Holm," cried a stern voice.

The man obeyed in momentary bewilderment. On the ground in front of him lay outstretched a splendidly built fellow, dressed in dirty rags. There he lay, weltering in blood and dirt, surrounded by empty bottles, with a red-blotched, swollen face, the original features of which nobody could guess. A stray beam of light from the distant street lamps was reflected, with a baleful, malicious gleam; in the orbits of his eyes.

Before this prostrate figure stood the man himself a tall fellow, of handsome build, clad in the same dirty raiment which the dead man wore. He stood before this other as his double.

Yet he was not completely a double, for he was a nothing-perhaps it is wrong to say a nothing ; he was an image of the other, such h might be seen in a mirror, an image that had stepped out of the glass, and now lived and moved.

He turned round hurriedly. There stood George, and he realised now that the latter, too, was nothing —only an image of the body that he once had possessed.

"O soul which lost command of your body, the very instant that the clock struck twelve on New Year's Eve," cried George, " you shall relieve me of my office ! For the space of a year. you shall liberate the souls from their earthly tenements."

At these words David Holm became his old aggressive self again. In a whirlwind of rage he rushed at the driver, made a snatch at his scythe to break it asunder-and at his cowl-to tear it to pieces. Then he felt his hands forced down, and his legs snatched from under him; something invisible was bound round his wrists, chaining them together, and likewise round his ankles. After that he was lifted up and flung roughly, as a dead thing, into the cart, and there he had to he, without anybody caring how he had fallen.

A moment afterwards the- cart started away !

CHAPTER IV
A CALL FROM THE PAST

It was a narrow and lofty, but fairly capacious, room in a suburban house —a house so small that it was completely taken up by this room and a smaller one, which served for a bedroom. The room was lighted by a lamp suspended from the ceiling, and by its gleam one could see that it was cosy and comfortable.

Not only that, it was a cheerful room, which provoked a pleasant smile on the lips of the visitor. You could see at once that those who dwelt there had amused themselves by furnishing it in such a way as to give the impression of its being a whole flat.

The entrance to it was in a side wall, and hard by the door stood a small stove. Here also was the kitchen, and in it was gathered together all that pertained to cooking. The middle of the room was furnished as a living-room, with a round dining-table, a couple of oak chairs, a tall grandfather's clock, and a little cupboard for china and glass. Here, of course, was the lamp, suspended from the ceiling, right over the round table, which sufficed to illuminate the ante-chamber —the innermost portion of the room-with its mahogany sofa and drawing-room table, its flowery Axminster rug, its palm-tree in a tasteful china pot, and the innumerable photographs!

What jokes such an arrangement of the furniture must have occasioned. If a good friend called, the fun would be to.take him into the ante-chamber and then apologise for his being left to sit by himself whilst his hostess was obliged to shut herself up in the kitchen. At the dinner-table —which stood so close to the cooking department that you could feel the warmth of the stove-you may have said many a time with great pomposity : " Now you may ring for the housemaid to take away the plates." And if one of the children began to cry in the kitchen, you might pretend to laugh at the joke that it should be careful not to shriek so loud, or. papa (who was sitting in the inner "room") might hear it.

Thoughts akin to these usually sprang to the minds of people .who saw the room, but to those who entered it on New Year's Eve, shortly after midnight, most assuredly no such light and flippant fancies occurred. Those who then entered it were two men, both so down at heel and ragged that they might have been taken for common tramps, if one of them had not been wearing a black robe over his rags, and holding in his hand a rusty scythe. It was an unusual get up for a vagabond, and, stranger still, was his way of entering the room-without turning a key or opening a door ever so little, but merely walking through it, although it was closed.

The second man was not wearing any alarming symbol, but when he came into the room, not walking, but in some queer fashion hauled and dragged in by his companion, he seemed a much more frightful object than the latter. Although he was bound hands and feet, and was with the uttermost contempt flung down on the floor by his companion, lying like a dark heap of rags and wretchedness, he inspired dread through the frantic wrath that flamed from his eyes and distorted his countenance.

The two men did not find the room empty when they entered. They saw, at the round table in the living-room part, a young man with weak features and a pretty babyish look about the eyes, sitting with a somewhat older but small and delicate woman. The man was wearing a jacket on which, in striking big letters across his chest, was embroidered the words Salvation Army. The woman was clad in black, without any symbol except a bonnet of the usual type affected by Slum-Sisters, which lay in front of her on the table and testified to her connection with the Salvationists.

Both these people were extremely distressed. The woman sat silently weeping, again and again drying her eyes with a moist and crumpled handkerchief. She did this impatiently, as if the tears embarrassed her by preventing her attending to something else that she ought to do. The man's eyes were also red with weeping, but, in the presence of another, he refrained from giving full vent to his grief.

Now and again they spoke a few words to each other, and it was evident that their thoughts were in another room with a sick person whom they had quitted for a moment so that her mother might be alone with her. They were, however, so engrossed with the invalid, that neither of them appeared to take the least-notice of the strangers. The latter certainly kept quite silent and still-the one standing erect, leaning against the door-post, the other lying nerve-racked at his feet. But the couple at the table ought, apparently, to have been amazed at these guests who had entered through closed doors and in the dead of night

At any rate, the man who was on the floor felt astounded that these people should turn their eyes from time to time in his and his companion's direction, without seeming to be aware of their presence. He, for his part, could see everything, and, when he had passed through the town, he had noticed that everything seemed just like he had seen it with his human eyes-yet no one appeared able to see him. In his frenzy, the man had nursed the thought of trying to scare; his enemies by revealing himself to them in his present state, but he was forced to admit that he could not render himself visible to them.

Never before had he been in this room, but he recognised both the people sitting at the table, and, for that reason, he had not the slightest doubt of his whereabouts. If anything could increase his rage, it was at being carried, against his will, to a place which he had, all the previous day, refused to enter.

Suddenly the Salvationist at the table pushed his chair back. " It is past midnight now," he said; "his wife thought that he would be back home by that time. I shall go there and ask him to come."

Saying this, he rose slowly and reluctantly from his chair and took up his coat, which was hanging at the back of his chair, to put it on.

"I understand quite well, Gustavsson, that you don't care for the job of going after him," replied the woman, struggling hard against the insistent weeping which threatened to stifle her voice, " but you must bear in mind,that it is the last favour Sister Edith asks of you."

The Salvationist paused just as he was putting his arm into his coat-sleeve. "Sister Mary," he said, "it may be true that this is the last service I can render Sister Edith, but I hope that David Holm will not be at home, or, if at home, that he will refuse to come with me. I have sought him several times to-day and begged him to come, as you and Captain Andersson told me to do, but I was glad all the time that he said ' No,' and that neither I nor anyone else succeeded in bringing him here."

The prostrate figure started, when he heard his name mentioned, and an ugly sneer spread over his face.

"That fellow seems to have a trifle more sense than the others," he mumbled. The Slum-Sister looked at the Salvationist, and spoke sharply, without her voice being choked with weeping. "Gustavsson, you had best this time convey the message in such a way that David Holm will be made to understand that he must come here! "

The Salvationist walked to the door with the air of a man who obeyed without conviction.

"Shall I bring him here, even if he is as drunk as drunk can be?" he asked from the door.

"Bring him here, Gustavsson-alive or dead, I had almost said. At the worst he can he here and sleep off his debauch. The only important thing is for us to get hold of him."

The Salvationist had laid his hand on the door handle when suddenly- he turned and walked back to the table.

"I don't like a fellow like David Holm coming here," he protested, and his face turned white with emotion. "Sister Mary, you know quite as well as I what sort of a fellow he is. Do you think, Sister, that he is fit to be here? Don't you think that he is far too foul to go in there ? " he continued, pointing to a door half-concealed in the ante-room part.

"Do I think " she began, but he did not let her finish what she had to say.

"Don't you realise, Sister Mary, that he may come only to jeer at us ? He will brag that one of the Slum-Sisters was so fond of him, that she could not die without getting a sight of him."

The Sister looked up suddenly and shaped her lips for a hasty retort, but she bit them together again and reflected.

"I can't bear his gossiping about her-least of all when she is dead !" exclaimed the Salvationist.

Directly afterwards came the Sister's answer, solemn and emphatic. " Gustavsson, are you certain that David Holm would be far wrong if he said that?"

The figure that lay imprisoned on the floor started, and was penetrated by a sudden feeling of joy. He was utterly astounded, and glanced up to George to see if he had noticed his emotion. The driver, however, stood motionless, but David Holm, by way of precaution, muttered something about it being a pity that he had not discovered that interesting fact while he was alive. It would have been something to brag about to his boon companions.

The Salvationist was so perturbed by what he had heard that he clutched hold of the arm of a chair. The walls of the room were dancing round him.

" Why do you speak in that way, Sister Mary ? " he asked" You don't want me to believe "

The Sister was a prey to strong emotion. She clenched her hand tightly round her handkerchief, while she uttered words which gushed forth in a wild torrent, as if she were in a hurry to get them said before hesitation came to stop her.

"Whom else should she hold dear? We two, Gustavsson, and all the rest who have learnt to know her, have allowed ourselves to be converted and conquered by her. We have resisted her in nothing, even up to the last. We have never mocked or sneered at her. She has no right to suffer either anguish or remorse for our sake. Neither you nor I, Gustavsson, is responsible for her lying where she now lies."

The Salvationist seemed calmed by this outburst.

"I did not realise that you were speaking of love for sinners, Sister."

"Nor do I, Gustavsson."

At this confident assurance, one of the spectres was again throttled by a feeling of joy which he could not express, but, afraid lest his anger, his frantic desire to rebel, should in some way be dispelled, he tried to choke it down at once. He had been taken by surprise, for up to now he had imagined that nothing but sermonising was in store for him. In future he intended to take better heed of himself.

Sister Mary sat down and bit her lips to overcome her emotion, y She was about to make a sudden plunge.

"It does not matter my speaking to you of that, Gustavsson," she began, for nothing matters now that she is about to die. If you will' sit down for a minute, I will explain what I mean."

The Salvationist wriggled out of his coat and resumed his seat at the table. Without uttering a word, he sat looking expectantly at the Sister with his fine, honest eyes.

"First of all, Gustavsson, I will tell you how we kept last New Year's Eve, Sister Edith and I, "she continued." It had been arranged at headquarters, in the previous, autumn, that a Slum Refuge should be established in this town, and we two were sent to start it. We had a fearful lot of work, but the Brothers and Sisters had done their utmost to help us, and by New Year's Eve we had got so far as to be able to move in. The kitchen and dormitories were already in order, and we had hoped that we should open the Refuge on New Year's Day itself-but that diti not come off, because the sterilising oven and the wash-house were not ready."

At first the Sister found it hard to keep from crying, but, as the story proceeded, and she was carried away from the present, her voice became more distinct.

" In those days you did not belong to the Army — if you had, you would have spent with us a very happy New Year's Eve. Some of the Brothers and Sisters paid us a visit, and we invited them to tea for the first time in the new home. You cannot imagine how happy Sister Edith was-at having established a Refuge here, where she was at home, and knew every poor person and understood what they needed. She walked about, looking at our coverlets and mattresses, our freshly painted walls, our bright pots and pans, with such joy that we could not help laughing at her. She was as merry as a grig-as the saying goes-and when Sister Edith is merry, then all the rest are merry."

"Halleluia! that I know," cried the Salvationist.

"The merriment lasted as long as our friends stayed," the Sister went on, "but after they had gone, a deep anguish overcame her at all the evil that exists in the world, and she said that I was to pray with her that it might not prevail against us. So we went on our knees and prayed for our Refuge, for ourselves, and for all those whom we hoped to succour. Just as we were kneeling in prayer, there came a ring at the front-door bell.

" Our friends had been gone but a very short time, so we said to each other that one of them had perhaps forgotten something, and wanted to fetch it; but, by way of precaution, we both went down to the street-door. When we opened it, we saw none of our friends, but one of those for whom the Refuge had been founded. There he stood in the doorway, big and ragged, but so drunk that he stumbled. He looked to me so awful that I was seized with terror, and thought that we ought to make the excuse that the Refuge was not yet opened, and decline to receive him. But 'Sister Edith was glad that God had sent her a guest — she thought that He wished by that to show us that He was looking favourably on our work. So she admitted the fellow. She offered him some supper, but he swore at her and said that he only wanted to he down. He went into a dormitory, and, after flinging off his coat, threw himself down on a camp-bed, and in another minute he was asleep."

"Fancy you being frightened of me ! " laughed David Holm to himself, but not without some hope, that the motionless figure behind him would hear that he was still the same David Holm as before. "It's a pity you cannot see me just as I am now — then methinks I should frighten the life out of you."

"Sister Edith wanted to show some exceptional kindness to the first person who came to our Refuge," the woman went on, " and I noticed that she felt disappointed when he went so promptly to sleep; but next moment she brightened up again, for she had just caught sight of his coat. Gustavsson, I don't think I have ever seen a garment so dirty, so ragged, and in such sorry plight as that was! It reeked so of filth and. Schnapps, Gustavsson, that it was hard to go near it. When I saw Sister Edith start to mend it, I could not help a dread coming over me. I told her to let it alone, as we had no oven or wash-house ready to disinfect it.

"You understand, Gustavssoni that this man was to Sifter Edith from the very first as a gift from God, and it was such a delightful task for her, to mend onl of his garments for him, that I could not prevent her. Nor did I help her either: No, I had said to myself, you know, that there might be infection in that coat-it-could not be right for me to touch such filth. She took the responsibility on herself, because I was her subordinate, and she saw that I did not undertake anything injurious to health ; but she set herself to sew and mend that coat the whole of New Year's Eve,"

The Salvationist on the other side of the table lifted up his hands and pressed them in ecstasy one against the other.

" Halleluia !" he cried; " thanks be to God and praise for Sister Edith!"

" Amen ! Amen ! " replied the Sister, beaming in a sudden ecstasy. " Thanks be to God and praise for Sister Edith-that is what we should always say, in sorrow as in joy. Thanks be to God and praise that she was what she was, to sit up all night bending over that horrible coat sewing at it as proudly and happily as if it had been a royal mantle."

He who had been. David Holm. felt a curious sense of rest and repose, picturing to himself the young girl, as she sat in the calm of night mending a poor vagabond's coat. After all that had been irritating and exciting him, there was something soothing and healing in this. If only old George had not been standing glum and motionless behind him, watching every movement of his, he would have liked to dwell long on this thought. " Thanks to God and praise," continued the woman, " that Sister Edith has never regretted that she sat up all that night, sewing on buttons and patching up holes, until four in the morning, without thinking of all the infection and stench she was inhaling. Thanks to God and praise that she never regretted sitting in a room so penetrated by the bitter chill of that winter's night that it became like an ice-house before she went to bed."

"Amen ! Amen ! " replied the Salvationist.

"She was quite frozen with cold when at last she was ready," remarked the Sister. "I heard how she lay and tossed and turned in her bed, for many weary hours, without being able to get warm. She had hardly dozed off when it was time to get up again, but I coaxed her into staying in bed and letting me look after the guest, in case he should get up before she had had her sleep out."

"Sister Mary, you have always been a good friend to her," replied the Salvationist.

"I know that it was a great privation for Sister Edith," she continued, with the ghost of a smile, "but she did it to please me. It was not long she lay in bed, for when the man had drunk his coffee, he asked me if it was I who had mended his coat. When I told him that it was, not, he asked me to fetch the Sister who had helped him.

"He was sober then, and quiet, and chose his words better than many of his stamp usually do, and, as I knew that it would be a great joy to Sister Edith to hear him express his thanks, I went to fetch her. When she came, she had not the look of one who had been awake all night, for she had a bright flush on her cheeks, and was so pretty in her joyful anticipation that the man was, to a certain extent, struck with admiration on seeing her. He had taken his stand by the door, and was waiting with such a baleful expression on his face that I was afraid he meant to strike her. ' There's no danger,' thought I, 'he won't do anything to her. Nobody could have the heart to hurt her."

" Halleluia ! Halleluia ! " chimed in the Salvationist. " But the fellow's face clouded again, and, when she came up to him, he tore so violently at the pilot coat he was wearing that the buttons-that had just been sewn on-were lugged out. After that he drove his hands so fiercely into his newly-mended pockets that we heard the cotton burst; and, last of all, he split up the fining of his coat till it hung in sorrier rags than when he had first come. ' You see, miss, I'm used to having it in that state,' the fellow jeered. ' It seems easier and most suitable for me. It was a pity, Sister Edith, that you should have given yourself so much trouble, but I can't help it.' "

The spectre which lay on the floor saw before him a face beaming with happiness, which was suddenly clouded. He almost acknowledged to himself that that silly monkey-trick of his had been cruel and ungrateful, when the thought of George again obtruded itself. " It is just as well that George should hear what sort of fellow I am-unless he knows it already," he decided. " David Holm is not the man to throw up the sponge at the outset. He is hard and wicked, and has a way of getting irritated by silly people."

"I had not before that moment given a thought as to how the fellow looked," continued the Sister, " but when he stood there and deliberately tore up what Sister Edith had sewn together with so many beautiful thoughts., I looked closely at him, and noticed that he was so tall and finely built that one could not help admiring such a handiwork of nature. He had, too, a good and easy carriage; his head was big and of the best shape ; his countenance at one time must have been handsome, though then it was so blotched and swollen that the features were undistinguishable, and one could not form an opinion as to how they may have looked at the beginning.

"Though he acted as he did, and, moreover, gave a loud and wicked laugh; though his eyes shone yellow and ferocious ; yet I think that Sister Edith only thought that she had met some special object for her charity, a human wreck far on the road to ruin. I noticed that at first she shrank back, as if she had been struck, but after that a bright fight illuminated her eyes, and she took a step nearer to the man.

" The only way she said was that, before he went, she wished to invite him to- come to her Refuge next New Year's Eve. And as he stood gazing at her in utter astonishment, she added: ' You see, I prayed to God to-night to grant to the first guest at this Refuge a happy New Year, so I want to see you again to find out if He has granted my prayer.

"As soon as he understood what she meant, the fellow broke out into oaths. ' Yes, that I promise you ! ' he jeered. ' I will come again and show you that He has not cared a rap for you and your namby-pamby nonsense.' "

The man who was thus reminded of a promise that he had made and quite forgotten, but had now, against his will, come to fulfill, felt for a moment like a weak reed in a strong man's hand, and wondered if his rebellion had any meaning. But he stifled the thought-he would not submit, he would fight until doomsday, if it was to be so.

The Salvationist grew more-and more excited while Sister Mary related this meeting on New Year's morning. He could not keep quiet any longer, but jumped up.

" You have not told me the name of that brutal tramp, Sister Mary-but I understand that it was David Holm! "

Sister Mary nodded assent.

" My God, my God, Sister Mary," he cried, outstretching both his.hands, " why will you insist on my fetching him here? Have you noticed any improvement in him since that morning? It seems as if you would have him here, so that she should see that her prayer to God had been made in vain. Why do you want to inflict such distress on her ? "

The Sister looked at him impatiently, almost angrily.

"I have not finished "

But the Salvationist interrupted her.

"We must take heed, Sister Mary, of the snare set by a lust for revenge. There is in me a being of sinful nature, who would- like to summon David Holm here, this very night, to show him the pure woman who is dying, and tell him plainly that-it is he alone who is responsible for her leaving us. I take it, Sister Mary, that it is your intention to tell David Holm that, while Sister Edith was carrying out the work which he, in his ingratitude, tore up, she caught a deadly infection. I have heard you say that she has never enjoyed a day's sound health since last New Year's Eve. We must take heed, Sister, we who have lived with Sister Edith and still have her in our sight, not to yield to the hardness of our hearts."

The woman bent over the table and spoke without looking up, just as if she had fitted her words to the figures on the tablecloth.

"Revenge?" she said. "Is it revenge to let a person understand that once he possessed some-thing most glorious, but that he has lost it ? Or, if I put a rusty iron into the fire to make it fresh and bright-is that revenge ? "

"I knew that it was so, Sister Mary," replied the Salvationist, with equal vehemence. " You hope to succeed in converting David Holm by laying on his conscience the burden of remorse. Have you ever seriously thought whether it might not be our own revenge that we are nursing and hugging to our hearts? There is a dangerous snare in that, Sister Mary. It is so easy to make a blunder."

The pale-faced Sister gazed on the man with eyes beaming with the rapture of self-denial, which said plainly enough : " To-night I am not seeding aught of my own."

The Salvationist turned red, tried to reply, but the words failed him. The next moment he flung himself down by the table bid his face in his hands, and, overcome by long-pent sorrow, began to weep.

The Sister did. not disturb him, but over her lips welled a prayer. " O Lord God, Jesus Christ, let US get through this miserable night. Grant me strength to help all my friends —I who am the weakest and understand least! "

The prisoner scarcely paid any attention to the charge of having infected Sister Edith, but he started when the Salvationist burst into tears. He had made a discovery which affected him strongly, and he hardly cared to hide it from the driver. It delighted him to realise that the girl whom that good-looking youth had loved preferred himself.

As the Salvationist's sobs became less and less violent, the Sister stopped praying.

"Gustavsson, you are thinking of what I said a little while ago about Sister Edith and David Holm."

A " Yes " was audible between his coat-sleeves, and at the same time the man's whole body quivered with pain.

" Gustavsson, that causes you much suffering, which I can well understand. I know another who has loved Sister Edith with all his soul-she herself remarked it and said that she could not understand it. She meant that if she were to care very much about a man, it would be one who stood higher than herself-and you think so too, Gustavsson. We can, I suppose, give our lives to help the wretched, but our purely human love we cannot give to any one of them. When I tell you that Sister Edith's love is given elsewhere, it wounds you."

The Salvationist did not move, but lay with his head against the' surface of the table. The invisible figure, on the other hand, made an attempt to get nearer, as if to hear better, but he was immediately ordered by the driver to keep quiet.

" If you move; David, I shall have to punish you in a way you have never dreamt of," he said, and David Holm, who now realised that the driver kept his word, and had strange powers, remained perfectly still.

" Halleluia! " shouted the Slum-Sister, with an excited expression on her countenance. " Halleluia! Who are we that we should judge her ? Have you not observed that, when a heart is filled with pride, it bestows its love on one of the great and mighty of this world; but when a heart is void of all but meekness and charity, to whom can it give its fondest love but to one who is greatest in cruelty and degradation, and has gone the farthest astray ? "

David Holm felt a prick of annoyance at these words. " You are very strange to-night," he thought to himself. " Why bother yourself about what those people say of you? Did you expect that they would value you very highly ? "

The Salvationist lifted up his head and looked as if he were putting to her a question. " It is not merely that, Sister Mary."

" Yes, Gustavsson, I understand what you mean —but you must bear in mind that Sister Edith did not know at the beginning that David Holm was a married man, and," she continued, after a slight hesitation, " anyhow, I think it hard to believe otherwise-all her love aimed at his conversion. If she had seen him standing on the platform, confessing that he was saved, she would have been happy."

The Salvationist grasped the Sister's hand, while he watched her lips attentively. At her last words he uttered a gasp of relief. " So it was not the love that I mean," he remarked.

The woman shrugged her shoulders .slightly and sighed at this obstinacy. " I have never received any confidence on this point from Sister Edith," she explained. "It may very well be that I am mistaken."

" If you have not heard anything from Sister Edith's own lips, then, in my opinion, you are mistaken," the young man stated very gravely.

The ghost, crouching by the door, grew gloomy; he did not like the turn the conversation had now taken.

"Gustavsson, I don't assert that Sister Edith felt anything but pity for David Holm the first time she saw him. And there was no reason either that she should have loved him afterwards-at one time he often came across her, and he persistently withstood her. Wives used to come to us and complain that their husbands had been enticed from their work since David Holm came to this town. And there was an increase of insolence, violence, and vice. Wherever we turned among the wretched we experienced it, and we fancied that we could always trace it to David Holm. But Sister Edith being what she is, it was quite natural that this very fact should make her more keen to win nim for God's sake. He was like a wild beast which she pursued with powerful weapons-the more the animal turned against her, the more doughtily she attacked it, confident that in the long run she would come off victorious, because it was she who was the stronger of the two."

" Halleluia ! " shouted her companion. " So she was, too, Sister Mary. Do you remember that you and Sister Edith went one evening to a public house, and walked round distributing notices of the new Slum Refuge ? On that occasion Sister Edith saw David Holm sitting at a table in company with a young man, who was listening to the fellow's jokes at the Slum-Sisters, and joined in his laughter. Sister Edith noticed that young man, and her heart was touched for him ; she whispered a few words to him about not letting himself be ruined. The young man did not answer her, nor did he follow her immediately-but he could not force a smile. Though he stayed in the same company, and filled his glass, he could not put it to his lips. David Holm and the others laughed at him and said that he had been frightened by the Sister. But that was not the case, Sister Mary, far 'from it; it was her compassion-that she could not help warning him-which touched the young man, and won him so that he must needs leave the others and follow her. You know this is a fact, Sister Mary, and you know also who the young man was.

"Amen I Amen ! It is true that I know who the man is who from that day became our best friend," replied the Sister, with a kindly nod to the Salvationist. " I don't deny that Sister Edith, got the better of David Holm on that occasion, but much more often she was worsted. She caught a chill that New Year's Eve, and she was always struggling with a cough that she could not get rid of-which she has not got rid of even to this very day. The despondency of sickness preyed on her, and that, maybe, was the cause of her not fighting with her usual success."

"Sister Mary," interrupted the Salvationist, " there is nothing in what you say that indicates that she was in love with him."

" No, Gustavsson, you are right; nothing indicated it at the beginning. I will tell you what made me think so. We knew a poor sempstress who had consumption, but who struggled against her disease, and, above all, fought with superhuman courage against spreading the infection. She had one child whom she wanted to save from contagion. She told us that, one day, when she was seized with coughing in the street, a tramp went straight up and abused her for the precautions she was taking. ' I also have consumption,' he said, ' and the doctor Wants me to be cautious-but not I! I cough right into people's faces, because I hope they will catch it and go to "Kingdom Come." Why should they be better off than we ? That's what I should like to know.' He said nothing else, but the sempstress was so frightened by him that she felt ill the whole day. She described him as tall, and of good appearance, though he was clothed in wretched rags. His face was indistinct to her, but for hours at a stretch she could see before her his eyes, which lay like two fierce yellow gleams , between swollen eyelids. What frightened her most was that he seemed neither drunk nor an. utter wreck, but nevertheless spoke as he did, and cherished such bitter hatred towards his fellow creatures.

" It was no wonder that Sister Edith recognised David Holm at once by this description, but what astonishes me is that she took up the cudgels for him. She tried to make the woman believe that he was only amusing himself by scaring her. ' It's quite out of the question that so strong a man as he should be in any way tuberculous,' she maintained. ' I think he is quite wicked enough to enjoy frightening you, but he is not depraved enough to infect people out of sheer malice, even if he were consumptive. He is certainly not such a monster.'

" We others contested this point-we believed that he was quite as bad as he had painted himself — but she defended him all the more warmly, and she was almost angry with us for thinking so badly of him."

For the second time the driver showed signs that he was observing what was going on around him. He bent down and looked into his companion's eyes. "I believe the Slum-Sister is right, David. She who could refuse, to credit everything evil of you must certainly have been very fond of you indeed."

"It may be, Gustavsson, that all that means nothing," continued the Sister, " and what I noticed two days afterwards even less. It happened one evening when Sister Edith returned home dejected —she was in low spirits at the woes that had befallen her charges-that David Holm came up and began talking to her. All he wanted was to tell her, he said in his sneering way, that she would have a better and a quieter time now, because he was going right away from the town.

"I expected that Sister Edith would have been glad at this news, but I perceived from her answer that she was unhappy about it. She told him straight out that she would prefer his staying-so that she might strive with him for some time longer.

"He said that he was sorry for this, but that he could not stay, however, because he was on a journey through Sweden in search of a person whom he absolutely must find. There would be no peace and quiet for him until he had found that person.

"You must know, Gustavsson, that Sister Edith inquired with such evident anxiety as to who this person was that I was nearly whispering to her to be careful not to give herself away to such a callous brute. He did not notice it, however, but simply replied that if he found the person in question she should be informed of it. He hoped that she would, be delighted that he need no longer tramp the wide, wide world as a poor vagabond."

"With this he departed, and he may have kept his word, for we saw nothing further of him. I hoped we should never have anything to do with him again, for he always seemed to me to bring bad luck wherever he appeared. One day, however, it so happened that a woman, came up to. Sister Edith at the Refuge and inquired for David Holm. She stated that she was Holm's wife, and had thrown him over, not being able to stand 'his drunkenness and bad habits. She had stolen away secretly, and taken her children with her, and come to our town, which lay far from their former home, and it had never entered his head to make any serious attempt to find her there. She had now got work in a factory, and was so well paid that she could support herself and her children. She was a welldressed woman who commanded confidence and respect. She was a sort of superintendent of the factory-girls, and had earned such good money that she was able to provide herself with a comfortable home, and a sufficiency of furniture and household utensils. Formerly, while she was still living with her husband, she had not possessed enough to feed herself and the children.

"She had now learnt that her husband had been seen in the town, that the Slum-Sisters knew him, and she had called on us to find out how he was going on.

"Gustavsson, had you been present then, and heard and seen Sister Edith, you would never have forgotten it. When the woman came and told us who she was, Sister Edith turned pale, and looked as if she had been stricken with mortal grief; but she quickly pulled herself together, and then a heavenly light shone in her eyes. It seemed as if she had gained a complete victory over herself, and cared nothing, for her own part, about earthly things. And, I must tell you, she spoke so beautifully to Holm's wife that she moved the woman to tears. She never uttered a word of reproach to her, yet she made her repent having deserted her husband. I believe she even got the woman to regard herself as a monster of harshness ! What is more, Gustavsson, Sister Edith contrived to revive the old love-the youthful love that the woman had felt for her husband when they were first married. She induced the wife to tell her about what sort of man he had been.during their early married days, and she got her to long for her husband. You must not think, Gustavsson, that she concealed what he was now, but she inspired the other woman with the same ardent desire to reform David Holm that she herself felt."

The driver, by the door, again stooped forward and observed his prisoner-but this time he rose without uttering a word. Something dark and horrible had gathered round his former friend, which he felt that he could not endure. He stretched himself at full length against the wall, and drew his cowl well over his eyes to escape seeing him.

"Certainly the wife already felt a germ of remorse for abandoning her husband to his wicked-ness and evil ways," the Sister went on. " It was whilst talking with Sister Edith that she received this new feeling. On this first occasion, however, there was no question about her duty to let the man know her address, but that was decided at the next long conversation'. And, Gustavsson, I won't insinuate that Sister Edith talked her over or gave her much hope, but I do know that she wanted the wife to invite him to her home. She thought that such an action might rescue him, and she did not dissuade the woman from it. I must say that that was Sister Edith's work, and that it came off ; I must say that it was she who united the man with those it was in his power to ruin. I have thought and wondered a good deal about that, and I do not understand how she dare venture to take on herself so grave a responsibility unless she had loved him."

The woman uttered these words in a tone of strong conviction, but the two, who' had been excited when she told of the sick Sister's love, now kept still. The Salvationist sat motionless, his hands over his eyes, and the figure prostrate at the door resumed the expression of black hatred which he bore when first he had been dragged into the room.

"None of us knew where David Holm had wandered to," continued the woman, "but Sister Edith sent him word by some tramps that we could give him information about his wife and children and it was not long before he came. Sister Edith brought him and his wife together, after she had seen to his being decently clothed, and had found him a job with some builders in the town. She exacted-no promise or undertakings, being aware that nobody can bind men of his sort by promises, but, as a good husbandman, she wanted to plant, in good new soil, the seed that had sprouted up amid thorns-and she was certain that she would succeed."

"Who knows if Sister Edith might not have been successful, if a great misfortune had not happened? To begin with, Sister Edith was attacked by inflammation of the lungs, and when that was subdued, and we were hoping for a speedy convalescence, she languished instead, and we had to send her to a sanatorium.

"I need not tell you how David Holm behaved to his wife-that you know as well as we do. The only person we have tried to keep in ignorance is Sister Edith herself, because'we wanted to spare, her feelings. We hoped that she would die without hearing of it, but. now I am not so sure. I think that she knows all. How could she have found out?

"The curious spiritual tie that unites her to David Holm is so strong, that I believe she may have gained information of what concerns him by other than the usual ways, and it is just because she knows all that she has been anxious the whole day to speak to him. She has brought endless misery on his wife and children, and she has but a few short hours in which to put things straight. And we are so helpless that we cannot assist her even by bringing him here."

"But what good would it do ? " demanded the Salvationist obstinately. "She can't talk to him-she is far too weak."

" I can talk to him in her name," replied the Sister confidently. " He would listen to my words, if spoken to him beside a death-bed."

"What would you say to him, Sister Mary ? Would you tell him that she loved him ? "

The Sister got up, clasped her hands across her breast, and stood with upturned face and closed eyes.

" Oh, Lord God ! " she prayed, " grant that David Holm comes here before Sister Edith dies ! Dear God ! vouchsafe that he may see her love, and that the fire of her love may melt his soul I Oh; God ! was not that love sent to her to melt his heart ? Good God, make me brave, so that I may not-think of sparing her, but dare to lay low his soul in the flame of her love! Oh, God ! let him feel it as a gentle breeze through his soul, as the breath from an angel's wing, as the red gleam that is kindled at dawn in the east and drives away the darkness of night. Let him not think that I would have vengeance on him, but make him understand that Sister Edith has loved the very soul in him —that which he himself has tried to choke and kill. Dear God —"

The Slum-Sister started and looked up. The Salvationist was putting on his coat once more.

" I will go after him, Sister Mary," he said, with a certain huskiness in his voice. " I will not come back without him."

But the prone figure by the door turned to the driver and addressed him.

"Haven't we had enough of this, George ? When I first came here there was; something that gripped me in what they talked about. In that way you might perhaps have softened me, but you should have warned them-they; should have avoided talking about my wife."

The driver did not answer, but with a slight gesture pointed towards the' room. A little old woman had entered through the hidden door, farthest away in the ante-room. She walked with silent steps to the couple who had been carrying on the long conversation, and spoke in a voice that quavered with the importance of the tidings she was about to announce.

"She will not he there much longer. Soon she will fly hither ! It will be over quickly now."

CHAPTER V
SISTER EDITH PLEADS WITH DEATH

The poor little Sister who was lying on her deathbed felt that she was getting weaker and weaker every moment. She was in no pain, but lay struggling against death, as, many a time, when she had been watching by- a sick-bed, she had struggled against sleep.

" Ah ! how sweet is the temptation ; but it will never do for you to overtake me." Such words 'had she addressed to sleep; if, at any time, it had descended on her for a couple of minutes, she had always jumped up quickly from it and returned to her duties.

Now she was thinking that, in some cool room-with a continual draught of pure frosted air that it would be a delight for her lungs to breathe —a bed, deep and broad, was spread, with pillows as soft and puffy as fermenting dough. She knew that this bed was arranged for her, and she longed to sink down in it and sleep off her physical weariness ; but she had a feeling that her sleep would be so sound that she would never wake again. She continued to resist the temptation of rest-that cannot fall to her lot as yet.

When the little Sister gazed round the room, there was a look of reproach in her eyes. She looked sterner than she had ever done before.

"How cruel you are not to help me with the only thing I long for," she seemed to explain. " Have I not gone out of my way many a time to serve you when I was well, cannot you now take the trouble to summon here the man I wish to meet ? "

More often than not she lay with her eyes shut, waiting and listening so intently that not a movement in the little house escaped her. Suddenly she received the impression that a stranger had entered the outer room, and was waiting to be shown in to her. She opened her eyes and looked imploringly at her mother.

"He is standing, you know, by the kitchen door. Can't you let him in, mother ? "

Her mother got up, went to the hidden door, opened it, and looked into, the bigger room. She came back, shaking her head.

"There is no one there, child," she said; "no one but Sister Mary and Gustavsson."

Then the sick girl sighed and shut her eyes again ; but she had still the feeling that he was sitting right against the door and waiting. If only her ^clothes had been lying, as usual, on a chair at the foot of the bed, she would have put them on, and gone herself to speak to him. But the clothes were not lying there,"and, besides, she feared that her mother would refuse permission for her to get up.

She wondered and wondered how she could manage to get into the outer room. She was certain that the man was there, but that her mother would not let him pass in to her-probably she thought that he looked awful, and did not want "to have anything to say to such a creature.

"Mother thinks that it is no good my meeting, him. She believes that it is a matter of indifference to me now I am fated to die."

At last, she hit upon a plan which seemed to her extraordinarily ingenious.

" I'll beg mother to let me move into the big room and he there," she decided. " I'll tell her that I long to see it once again Mother cannot have any objection to that."

She expressed her wish, but could not help wondering if her mother had seen through her proposal of changing her room, for the elder woman had so much to urge against it.

"Are you not lying comfortably where you are ? " the woman asked. " You were pleased enough, you know, to He here on other days."

She did nothing to gratify the sick girl's wish. The little Sister felt as if she were a child again, and had begged her mother for something that the latter did not consider proper to give her ; and, in the same way, like a little child, she now began imploring and worrying, so as to exhaust her mother's patience.

" Mother, I should so dearly like to go into the big room. Gustavsson and Sister-Mary will carry me there, if only you will call them. It won't be for long, mother, that my bed need remain there." "You shall find," replied' the mother, "that you will no sooner be there than you will want to come back here again ! " But she got up and : quickly returned with, the two friends.

It was fortunate that Sister Edith was lying in the little wooden bedstead which she had slept in as a child, so that the three-Gustavsson, Sister Mary, and her mother-could manage to carry her out. Directly she was in the larger room, she cast a glance towards the kitchen-corner, and was quite astounded at not seeing Holm there — for this time she felt quite sure that she was right.

She felt cruelly disappointed, and, instead of looking about her in the three-partitioned room which held so many memories, she shut her eyes. Once again she had the feeling that a stranger was lingering by the door.

"It's impossible that I can be mistaken," she thought; " somebody must be there-he or some-one else."

She opened her eyes and examined the room with the closest scrutiny. Then, by dint of great pains, she discovered that " something " was standing by the door-not so visible as a shadow, but what she called the shadow of a shadow.

The mother bent over her affectionately. "Are you feeling more restful now that you are in here ? "

The girl nodded, and whispered that she was so glad to be there ; but she was not thinking of the room, but lay all the time gazing at the door.

"What is that over there ? " she wondered, and deemed it' more than a matter of life and death to find out.

They had placed her bed in that part of the room which she and her mother used to call their drawing room, and this part was farthest from the door. After she had been lying there for a short time she whispered to her mother : " Now that I have seen how it looks in the drawing-room, I should like to go into the dining-room."

She noticed her mother exchanging a worried glance with the other two, and the shaking of their heads. ' This she interpreted as their fear of moving her nearer to that shadow which was lingering by the threshold. She had now, little by little, begun to suspect who he was, but she had no dread of him, but only wanted to get nearer to him.

She glanced imploringly at her mother and friends, and they obeyed her without further demur.

When she found herself in the central part that they used to call the dining-room she was much nearer the door, and could discern a dark form lingering there, with some sort of imple-ment in his hands. It could not be David Holm, but it was someone whom it was imperative that she should meet, the girl decided.

She must get nearer still to him ; so, while she tried hard to force an apologetic smile, she also showed by signs that she wanted to be carried into the " kitchen." She observed that her-mother was so saddened by this that she began to weep, and through her mind flitted the thought that her mother was calling to mind her sitting in the kitchen in front of the stove, her face flushing in the fire-glow, and herself chattering about everything that had happened to her at school, her mother meanwhile preparing their supper. She realised that her mother was actually thinking that she saw her child in her usual places, and was reefing under the feeling of emptiness that sweeps over her. But she must not think any more about her mother now, nor fix her attention on aught but the one important task which she must accomplish within the little time that remains to her.

When she had been moved to the farthest part of the room she could at last see quite dis-tinctly the invisible form by the door. It was a figure clad in a black habit, his head and face hidden by a cowl. In his hand he held a long scythe. Sister Edith did not doubt for an instant who he was.

"It is Death," she thought, and she was afraid that he had come too soon for her; otherwise he did not alarm her at all.

While the poor sick girl had been drawing nearer and nearer, the prone and prisoned figure had been crouching and trying to make itself smaller, as if he wished to escape her notice. He observed that she was incessantly looking towards the door, and it seemed to him that she saw something there. He did not want her to see him ! That would be far too great a humiliation for him to suffer. Nor did her glances meet his; they were directed at another; and he realised that if she did indeed perceive anyone, it was not he, but George.

She had hardly got as near as possible to them before he observed that she was calling George to her by a little sign with her head. George pulled his cowl down lower than before, as though he were deadly cold, and approached her. She looked up at him with a smile.

"You see that I am not afraid of you," she whispered, inaudibly to the living watchers in the room. "I will, willingly obey your summons, but I must first ask if you can grant me a delay till to-morrow, so that I may accomplish the great task for which God sent me into this world."

Whilst she was thus occupied in talking to George, David Holm lifted up his head so as to see her. He noticed that the holy exaltation of her soul had bestowed on her a beauty she had never possessed before-something lofty, unattainable, but so irresistibly winning that. he could no longer think of taking his eyes off her.

"Perhaps you cannot hear me?" she said to George. "Bend further over me. I must speak to you without the others hearing what I say."

George bent down until his cowl nearly brushed her face. " Speak as low as you like; I shall even then hear you."

She began to speak in a whisper so weak that none of the three around her bed had an inkling that she was saying anything at all. It was only the driver and the other spectre who heard her.

" I don't know if you are aware of what that means to me," she continued to George, " but I am in dire need of a delay till to-morrow so that I may meet someone whom I must put in the right way. You do not know how ill I have acted. I have been too arbitrary, too presumptuous. How can I stand before the face of God, I who am the cause of so dreadful a misfortune ? "

Her eyes dilated with fright, and she drew a deep breath, but proceeded without waiting' for an answer.

" I must, I suppose, tell you that he whom I want to meet is the man I love. You understand me, don't you? The man I love."

" But, Sister," replied the driver, " the man "

But she would not hear his answer, until she had put before him all that ought to move him.

" You understand that I am in dire need when I say this. It is not easy for me to confess that I love that particular man. It has shamed me to think that I must be so abandoned as to love one who is bound to another. I have striven and fought against it; I have felt that I, who should be a guide and example to the outcasts, am become worse than the worst among them."

One hand of the driver stroked her brow to calm her, but he uttered not a word, and allowed her to proceed with her, story.

"But the bitterest humiliation does not he, after all, in my loving a married man! My lowest degradation is that he whom I love is a wicked man. I don't know why I should have thrown myself away on a scoundrel. I hoped and trusted that some good might be found in him, but I have been deceived again and again. I must myself be bad, since my heart could go so far astray. Oh! can you not understand that it is impossible for me to depart, before I have made yet another attempt, without my having seen him become another and a different man ? "

"But you have made so many attempts already," remarked Red George doubtfully.

She shut her eyes and considered, but soon looked up again, and now a new assurance gleamed from her countenance.

"You think that I am asking for my own sake, and you believe, like the rest, that it does not matter what becomes of him. I shall, however,be taken away from everything here below. I beg leave to speak to you about something which has happened this very day, so that you may understand that it is to help others that I need the delay."

Sister Edith closed her eyes, and continued talking without opening them.

"Well, it was in the forenoon. I don't exactly understand how it could be so, but I was out with a basket on my arm, presumably about to take food to some poor person. I was standing in a yard where I know that I have never been before. There were many tall houses round me, and they looked respectable and in good condition, as if they were inhabited by well-to-do people. I did not know what I could possibly have to do in that quarter, but I noticed that there was an outbuilding against the wall of a house, which seemed originally meant for a fowl-house. But somebody had tried to transform it into a human dwelling. Bits of boards and card were nailed on to it; it had a few crooked windows, and two chimneys of sheet iron on the roof.

"Thin smoke issued from one of the chimneys, and from that I understood that the place was inhabited. Said I to myself : 'It is here, of course, that I am going.' I walked up a flight of wooden stairs, which were as steep as a ladder, and which more than once gave me the impression that I was climbing to some sort of bird's nest-and then I put my hand to the lock. I felt that it was unlocked, and, on hearing voices within, I entered without knocking.

"No one turned round and looked at me when I entered, so I withdrew to a corner by the door, and stood waiting till I should be wanted, for I knew, for certain, that I had come there for some specially important purpose. Meanwhile I stood thinking that I had come into an outhouse, and not into a room for human beings. There was scarcely a stick of furniture, not even a bed. In a corner lay some ragged mattresses which might conceivably serve for beds. No chairs-at any rate, none that any dealer would look at-and only one clumsy unpainted table.

"Suddenly I said to myself that I knew my whereabouts. It was David Holm's wife who was standing in the middle of the room. They must, therefore, have moved whilst I was at the sanatorium. Why were their circumstances so uncomfortable and wretched ? And where was their furniture ? Where were the beautiful chiffonier and sewing machine and — — I stopped reckoning, not knowing what I did not miss. In fact, there was simply nothing.

" ' How full of despair the woman looks,' thought I, ' and how poorly she is clad. She is not the woman she was last spring.' I wanted to run up and ask her, but was prevented because there were two strange ladies in the room engaged in an animated conversation with David Holm's wife. They were very serious, all three, and I soon got to know the subject of their conversation-that the poor woman's two children were to be taken to a children's asylum, to prevent their being infected by the father, who had consumption.

"One thing which I could not understand was their speaking of two children —I seemed to remember that there had been three. It was not. long before I learnt the reason. One of the benevolent ladies noticed that the poor woman was crying, and said something in a kind way about the children being as well cared for in the asylum as in any private home.

"Doctor, you must not mind my crying,' I heard the wife reply; ' I should cry worse if I had not to send the children away. I have the youngest of them at the hospital. When I saw how he suffered, I said to myself that if I could get the other two away from home I would not say a word against it, but only be too glad and grateful.'

" When she said this, I felt profoundly depressed. What had David Holm done to his wife, his home, and his children-or, to put it more precisely, what had I done ? It was I who had inflicted him on them. I began to cry and sob in the corner where I stood. I could not make out why the others did not observe me, but not one of them seemed to do so.

" I saw the wife approach the door. ' I will go down to the street and call the children in,' she said ; ' they are not far away.' She went past me and came so close that her poor patched clothes brushed against my hand. Then I fell on my knees, drew her dress to my lips, and wept, but not a word could I utter-the wrong that I had done this woman was far too great for that. I was astonished that she should not observe me, but I could well understand her not having any wish to speak to one who had brought such dire misfortune on her home.

" The poor mother, however, did not leave the room, because one of the ladies told her that there was a matter that must be settled before the children were called in. She took a paper out of a handbag and read aloud from it. It was a certificate stating that the parents entrusted their children to her care, for so long as their home was infected with tuberculosis, and it had to be signed by both father and mother.

" There was a door in the opposite side of the room ; it opened now and David came in. I could not help thinking that he had been waiting behind this door, so as to put in an appearance just at the right moment. He was dressed in his old shabby clothes, and he had a wicked gleam in his eyes. I could not help saying to myself that he looked about him with obvious delight, as if he were rejoicing in all the misery round him. He began talking about how much he loved his children, and how hard he felt it, after one of them had been taken to the hospital, to lose the two others also.

"The two ladies scarcely troubled to listen to him, but simply remarked that it was much more certain that his children would be lost to him, unless he sent them away from him. His wife had drawn herself up against a wall, and she was looking at him, so I thought, as one who had been beaten and tortured might look at her tormentor. It began to dawn on me that I had acted worse than I had hitherto thought. It seemed to me that there mus£ be a secret hatred of the woman in David Holm, and that he had sought to be reconciled with her, not from his longing for a home, but in order to torment her.

"I heard him entertain these cultured ladies with a speech about his paternal love. They replied that he could best prove it by observing the doctor's orders, and not infecting those around him, which would be the case, they saw clearly, if the children were kept at home. But none of them yet had an inkling of what he had in mind. It was I who first understood it. ' He means to keep the children,' thought I;' he does not trouble about their catching 'the disease.'"

The wife had just realised it. She shrieked violently, distractedly. That murderer! He won't let me send them away; he means them to stay at home for him to give them consumption, that they may die. In this way he has calculated to be revenged on me.'

" David Holm turned away from her with a shrug of his shoulders. 'It is a fact that I will not sign the paper,' he said to the two ladies. There was some angry talk and attempts at persuasion. The wife stormed at him with words of fury, and even the faces, of the two ladies flushed deeply; cutting things were said !

"But David Holm stood there quite calmly, and said that he could not do without his children. I listened to this with indescribable anguish. None of the others could suffer as I did, because none of them loved the man who was committing this foul deed. I stood there, hoping that they would find the right words to move him to compassion. As to myself, I wanted to rush out of my corner; but a curious feeling of being fastened down came over me. I was unable to stir. ' What use is it to dispute or try persuasion ? ' thought I. ' With a man such as he, the only course is to frighten him.' Neither his wife nor either of the others said a word about God; no one threatened him with the wrath of God's justice. I thought that I was holding God's punitive thunderbolt in my hand, but was powerless to hurl it!

" Once more there was silence in the room. The two ladies got up to go ; they had accomplished nothing, nor had the wife either. She had ceased making a fight, and had collapsed in despair. I made a superhuman effort to move and speak. The words burned my tongue. ' Oh, you hypocrite ! ' I wanted to say, ' Do you think that I do not know the purpose you have in view ? I, who am a dying woman, summon you to meet me before God's judgment seat! I accuse you before the Supreme Judge of intending, to murder your own children. I shall bear testimony against you.'

"But when I got up to say this I was no longer there, in David Holm's dwelling, but at home lying helpless in my bed ! After this I called and called, but could not get him here."

The little Slum-Sister had lain with her eyes shut all the while she was whispering this story. Now she opened them wide, and looked at George with unutterable anguish.

"You cannot really let me die without having spoken to him ? " she implored. " Think of his wife and children ! "

The crouching figure marvelled over George. He could have calmed the dying girl by a single word-told her that David Holm was out of the game, and could no longer injure wife and children. But he concealed this piece of news from her, and, instead, made her even sadder than she was already.

"What influence could you have over David Holm? " he asked. " He is not a man to let his heart be softened. What you have seen to-day is nought else than the revenge he has cherished in his heart for long years."

" Oh, don't say that, don't say that! " Sister Edith cried.

" I know him better than you do," replied the driver," and I will tell you what it was that made David Holm the man he is now."

"I should like to hear that," she said ; " it would be good for me if I could get to understand him."

"You must accompany me to another town," said the driver, "and we must stand outside a prison cell. The time is evening, and a man who has been confined for a week or two for drunkenness has just been released. No one is waiting for him at the prison gates, but he stands there staring about him in the hope that someone will come — for he had been looking forward to having a jolly time just then.

" It so happens that the man who is coming out of prison has just been subjected to a terrible shock, for while he was interned his younger brother turned out very badly. He had committed manslaughter whilst in a state of intoxication, and had been sent to goal for it. The elder brother knew nothing of the affair, until the gaol chaplain took him to the culprit's cell, and showed him the man sitting there with his handcuffs still on him —for he had been violent when taken to the gaol. Do you see who is sitting there? asked the clergyman, and when the man saw that it was his brother, he was deeply affected, because he had always been very fond of him. ' Here is a man who will have to remain in prison for a great many years,' said the clergyman, ' but we all say here, David Holm, that it is you who ought by rights to be undergoing the punishment, instead of him, for it is you, and nobody else, who tempted him and led him astray, till he became such a sot as not to know what he was about.'

" It was all David Holm could do to keep himself calm till he returned to his cell, but then he began to weep as he had never wept since he was a child. Afterwards he said to himself that he meant to turn away from his evil courses. He had never realised before that he had brought great misery on one he cared for. Then his thoughts turned from-his brother to his wife and children, and suddenly he realised that they, too, had had a rough time, but now he vowed to himself that never again should they have cause to complain of him. That very evening of his coming out of prison he longed to tell his wife that he intended turning over a new leaf.

"But she did not meet him at the prison gate, nor did he meet her on the road. Even when he reached their dwelling and knocked, she did not open wide the door to him, as she did at other times when he had been away for long. He had a suspicion of how things were, but refused to credit it. It is impossible that this should happen now, at the very time when he intended becoming another man.

" His wife always used to push the key under the door-mat when she went out. He stooped down and found it in the usual place. He opened the door, looked into his little home, and wondered if he had gone mad, because the room was quite empty-well, not exactly empty, for most of the furniture was still there, but not a living creature.

"Nor was there any food or fuel, or curtains to the windows-the room was comfortless, raw, and cold, and did not seem to have been lived in for many days past. He went to the neighbours and inquired if his wife had been ill while he was away. He tried to persuade himself that she had been taken to the hospital. ' Oh, no, there was nothing the matter with her lately, when she went away/ they replied. ' But where has she gone to ? ' Ah ! nobody knew that.

"He saw that they were curious, and maliciously glad at his discomfiture, and he recognised that there was only one explanation-that his wife had taken advantage of the opportunity, whilst he was in prison, to go her own way, taking with her the children and whatever else she chiefly needed, and made no preparations for him, but let him return home to all this bareness and desolation. And he had anticipated coming to her with such joy. He had rehearsed what he was going to say to her, for he really meant to ask her forgiveness. He had a chum, a young fellow who had belonged to a cultured class of society, but was quite ruined. He intended to promise to drop associating with him, although he was attracted to him not only, for the evil in him, but also because he had learning and science. On the following day he meant to go to his old employer and ask to be taken on again. He would have slaved for her and the children, so that they should get nice clothes to wear, and never have another anxious moment. And now, when he had thought out all this, she had run away from him !

" He grew hot and cold, by turns; he shivered over her heartlessness. Yes ! he could have understood her going, if it had been done openly and honourably, in which case he would have had no right to be enraged, for she had had a hard life with him. But she had stolen away, and let him return to an empty home without any warning, which was heartless. Never could he forgive her for that.

"He had been put to shame before all his fellows; he was, in fact, the laughing-stock of 'the whole neighbourhood. But he swore that he would put a stop to their laughter. He would find his.wife yet, and then he would make her as wretched as he was himself-nay, twice as much ! He would teach her how it felt to freeze, as he did, to the " very heart core.

"It was the only comfort he could indulge in-the thought of how he would punish her when he found her. Since then he had been hunting for her for three years, and all the time he had fostered his hatred with the thought of what she had done to him, till it became a crime of the highest magnitude. He had gone alone on lonely ways, and, as time went on, the greater grew his hate and lust for vengeance. He sought after her so long that he succeeded admirably in devising how he could torture her if ever they came together again."

The little Slum-Sister had kept silent till now, but she had followed the story with features betraying every emotion. Now, in an agonised voice, she interrupted the dark figure.

"Oh, no ! Say nothing more ; it is too dreadful! How shall I ever be able fo answer for what I have done ? Oh ! that I had not brought them together! If I had not, his sin would not have been so great."

"No, I need say nothing more," replied the driver. "I only want you to understand that it is useless your asking for a delay."

"Oh, but I want it ! " she exclaimed. " I cannot die, I cannot. Give me but a few moments. You know that I love him, have never loved him so. much as I do to-day."

The spectre on the floor gave a start! All the time Sister Edith and the driver had been conversing he had been gazing at her. He had absorbed every word of hers, and every expression of her countenance, so that he might remember them for ever. All that she had said, even when she had been most severe against him, had been a joy for him to hear ; her anguish, too, and her sympathy, when George was relating his history, had healed his wounds. He hardly knew as yet by what name to express his feelings for her; all he realised was that he could bear anything from her. He knew this-that her loving such a creature as he was, who had brought her to death's door, was something supernaturally splendid! Every time she stated that she loved him, his soul experienced an ecstasy which he would never have thought possible. He tried hard to attract the driver's attention, but the latter never looked in his direcrtion. He tried to rise, but tumbled back in unspeakable torments.

He noticed how restlessly and with what anguish Sister Edith moved in her bed. She stretched out to George her hands folded in prayer, but his face was stern and implacable.

"I would grant you a delay, if delay could help you," he said to her, " but I know that you have no influence over the man."

With these words, the driver stooped down to utter the words that were to release the soul from its bodily cover.

At that very moment a dark figure crept painfully along the floor to the dying girl. With a tremendous effort, and at the cost of a pang the like of which he could never have had. the slightest conception, he had sundered his bonds in order to reach her. Although he believed that he would be punished by these pangs throughout eternity, nevertheless Sister Edith should not grieve and long in vain when he was in the same room. He stole up to the other side, where George could not see him, and he got far enough to be able to grasp one of her hands.

Although it was impossible for him to exert the slightest pressure on this hand, yet, nevertheless, she was conscious of David's presence; and, by a sudden movement, she turned towards him. She saw him kneeling by her side-ah ! and what is more, with his face pressed to the floor, as he did not dare to look up at her, but, by the hand that embraced hers, he endeavoured to express to her his love, his gratitude, and the tenderness which was springing up in his heart.

A gleam of most blissful happiness spread over her countenance ; she looked up at her mother and her two friends-to whom she had not yet had time to say a farewell word-so as to gain their sympathy with the splendid thing that had happened to her ! She pointed her free hand to the ground, so that they might see and share her endless joy over David Holm, lying contrite and remorseful at her feet.

But at that instant the spectre, clad in black, leant towards her, and spoke : " O captive, O beloved one, come forth from thy prison ! "

The girl threw herself back on her pillows, and life left her in a sigh.

At the same moment David Holm was snatched away. The bonds which he could not see, but only feel, tightened once more round his arms, while his feet were left free. George made him understand, in an angry whisper, that he would have been punished with eternal sufferings had it not been for their old friendship's sake.

" Come with me hence at once," he went on ; " we two have nothing further to do here. They who have to receive her are come."

He dragged David Holm out with extreme violence. The latter thought that he saw the room suddenly filled with bright figures. He seemed to meet them on the stairs, and in the street-but he was whirled away at such a giddy pace that he could not distinguish them.

CHAPTER VI
THE OLD WOMAN ON THE ROADSIDE

David Holm was lying nerve-racked in the death-cart, wrathful, not against the whole world, but against himself. What frenzy had lately seized him? Why had he thrown himself at Sister Edith's feet, like a penitent and remorseful sinner ? George must certainly he laughing at him. A man, if he was deserving of that name, ought to stand by his deeds-he knew why he had committed them. He would not rush off and fining everything he had overboard, merely because a bit of a girl said that she was in love with him. Was it love? But he was dead-she was dead! What kind of love could that be?

The lame horse was moving again, jogging down one of the streets which led out of the town The houses became fewer and fewer, the street lamps farther apart. The boundary of the town was in sight and then these objects would cease.

As they were approaching the last lamp-post Holm was seized by a land of depression, a vague anxiety to get right away from the town. He felt that he was being taken from something which he ought not to leave.

At the very moment that he felt this disquiet, he heard, amid all the indescribable creaking and rattling of the cart, a voice speaking behind him, and he lifted his head to listen.

It was George, in conversation with someone who seemed to be riding with them in the cart — a passenger whom he had not noticed up to now. "I must not accompany you farther," said a gentle voice, so choked by pain and sorrow that it was scarcely audible. " I had so much to tell him, but he is lying "here angry and malicious, and I cannot make myself either seen or heard by him. You must please let him understand from me that I have been to meet him, but I am being carried away from this town, and must never again appear to him as I am now."

"But suppose he repents and regrets ? " asked George.

"You yourself have said that he can repent of nothing," replied the voice in a sorrowful tremor.

"You must tell him from me that I thought we should belong to each other for eternity, but now from this moment he can never see me again."

"But if he can make atonement for his evil deeds? " George queried.

" You will kindly tell him from me that I was ' not allowed to accompany him farther than here," wailed the voice, "Bid him farewell from me."

" But if he can reform and become another man ? " George insisted.

" You may tell him that I shall always love him," replied the voice, in a strain of greater melancholy than before. " I have no other hope to give him."

David Holm had got on his knees at the bottom of the cart. At these words he made a violent effort, and suddenly stood upright at full length. He snatched at a " something " which fluttered away from the uncertain clutch of his manacled hands-he did not succeed in clearly distinguishing what it was, but it left an impression of something gleaming bright, of a beauty beyond all dreams.

He wanted to tear himself free and dash after the fugitive, but was prevented by something that paralysed him more than mere fetters and bonds.

It was love-the love of spiritual beings, of which earthly love is but a poor imitation-which once again overmastered him, as at the death-bed. It had slowly burnt through him, just as a fire whilst it is burning up, slowly burns the wood into a glow. Scarcely anyone notices its action, but nevertheless, " from time to time, it sends out a sudden flame to show that it is about to set the whole ablaze.

Such a sudden flame was that which now blazed up within David Holm. It did not gleam in full radiance, but its light was sufficient for him to see the beloved one in such glorious guise that he must needs sink down stricken by helplessness-conscious that he dare not, that he had not the will, that he could not endure to approach her.

The driver's cart continued its way in pitch darkness. On either side stood a dense and towering forest; so narrow was the road that the sky was indistinguishable. It seemed to Holm that the horse was moving, more slowly than ever, the creaking of the wheels was more piercing, his own self-examination more strict, and the forlorn monotony, greater than in other spots. Then George drew in the reins, for a moment the creaking ceased, and the driver cried aloud in a high-pitched voice.

" What is all the torture I am suffering, what are all the. torments that await me, compared to the uncertainty of the only thing which is of vital importance to know? I thank thee, O God, that I am come from the darkness of mortal life. I praise and glorify Thee in all my misery, because I know that Thou hast bestowed on me the gift of eternal life."

The journey was resumed with jolts and creaking, but the driver's words long lingered in David Holm's ears. It was the first time he had felt some little sympathy with his old friend.

" He is a brave man," he thought; " he does not complain, although there is no hope of his getting away from his occupation."

It was a long journey, this ; one that seemed never to reach an end.

After they had journeyed so long that David Holm supposed they had been on the road for a day and a night they reached a wide plain which was overshadowed by a sky no longer sullen but clear, and then a half-moon glided up between the Three Wise Men and the Pleiades.

With creeping slowness the lame horse jogged over the plain, and when at last it was crossed David Holm looked up at the moon's disk to find out how far it had got. Then he observed that it had not moved at all, and he began wondering at this!

They journeyed on and on. At long intervals he glanced up to the sky, and saw that the moon never stirred from her place between the Three Wise Men and the Pleiades, but remained still.

At last he realised that, although he had supposed that they had been journeying for a day and a night, yet no change had taken place from night till morning nor from day to evening, and that there had been the same night all the time.

For hours and hours, so it seemed to him, they journeyed on, but on heaven's great dial none of the Wise. Men had moved-everything remained in its old position.

He might have thought that the world had stayed its course if he had not remembered what George had told him about time being stretched out-stretched out so that the driver might reach all the places he had to reach. He realised with a shudder that what for him was drawn out to days and days and nights and nights might not be more than one short moment, according to man's reckoning of time.

In his childhood he had heard speak of a man who had visited the blessed in heaven in their dwellings. When the man came back he said that a hundred years in God's heaven had passed as quickly as a single day on earth. But for him who drove the death-cart perhaps a single day was as long as hundreds of years on earth. Again he felt a touch of sympathy for George.

"It is no wonder that he longs to be released. It has proved a long year to him."

Whilst driving up a steep hill, they caught sight of a person who was travelling even slower than themselves, and whom they would overtake.

It was an old woman, bent and decrepit, who got along by the aid of a substantial stick, and who, despite her feebleness, was carrying a bundle so heavy that it quite dragged her down on one side.

It seemed as if the old woman had the faculty of seeing the death-cart, for she made way for it, and stood still by the roadside when it came right opposite her. Afterwards she slightly quickened her pace so that she could keep up with the cart, and meanwhile she eyed it very closely to find out what manner of thing it was.

In the clear moonlight it was not long before she observed that the horse was an old one-eyed crocks that the harness was fastened together with birch twigs and bits of string, that the cart was worn out, and in chronic danger of losing both its wheels.

" It is extraordinary that anybody should venture to drive about in a vehicle of that description and with such a horse," mumbled the old woman to herself, without thinking that the travellers might hear her. " I was thinking of asking a lift for a bit of the way, but that poor horse has all it can do to get along, and the cart might break to pieces if I stepped into it."

She had, however, hardly spoken the Words before George leaned over his seat and began to sing the praises of his horse and cart.' " Ah I " said he, " this cart and horse are not so bad as you think. I have driven them over roaring seas, where the waves rose as high as horses, and great ships sank, but they have not overturned with me."

The old woman was somewhat dumbfounded, but she decided that she had come across a carter who liked to have his little joke, and she' was not long in giving him tit for tat.

" Perhaps there are some who get on better on the roaring seas than they do on dry land," she said, "for I am inclined to think that they will find it a bit awkward to make progress here,"

"I have driven through precipitous mine-shafts right down into the bowels of the earth," said the driver, " without the horse stumbling-and I have driven through burning towns where it has been like a blast furnace, with fire on all sides. No fireman has ventured so far through fire and smoke as that horse has gone without shying."

" You like making merry over an old body, driver," retorted the old crone.

"Sometimes I have had business on the highest mountains, where no beaten track existed," continued the driver, " but the horse has climbed up mountain-walls and ventured over chasms, and yet the cart has stood it-though the ground on these places was nothing but a succession of blocks of stone. I have journeyed over marshes where there was no solid turf, that could bear a child, and snow which lay in drifts as high as a man, and it has not been able to stop me-so I don't think I can complain of my gear."

"Well, if it is as you say, I don't wonder you are pleased," remarked the old woman, agreeing with him. " You are, I can see, a real swell, you with your fine horse and carriage! "

"I am the strong one who has might over the children of men," replied the driver, and his voice took a deep and solemn tone. " I bring them under my sway, whether they dwell in lofty halls or in wretched cellars. I bestow freedom on slaves, and I tear down kings from their thrones. There is no citadel so strong but I can scale its walls ; there is no science so profound that avails to arrest my progress. I smite the confident, however much they bask themselves in the sun of prosperity, and I bestow wealth and possessions on the wretched who have languished in poverty."

"Didn't I guess," said the old woman, laughing, " that I had come across some big-wig ? But since you are so grand and have such a fine carriage, perhaps you could give me a lift ? I was off to one of my daughters for New Year's Eve, but I missed my way, and I believe I shall have to spend the whole night walking on the King's highway, unless indeed you will be good enough to help me."

"No, you must not ask me for that," cried the driver. "You will fare better on the road than if you were in my cart."

"Well, I dare say you are right there," said the old woman. " I rather think your horse would stumble if he had to carry me ; but, anyhow, I'll put my bundle in the back of the cart; I fancy you could help so far."

Without asking further leave, she shifted her bundle and deposited it on the bottom of the cart-but at sank down to the ground without the slightest stop, just as if she had put it on belching smoke, or on driving mist.

Maybe at that very moment she lost sight of the cart, for she remained standing in the road, bewildered and trembling, without attempting to resume her talk with the driver.

But this conversation made Holm more sympathetic with George. " He has certainly had to go through a good deal," he thought; " I am not surprised that he is so altered."

CHAPTER VII
THE STRUGGLE OF A SOUL

George carried David Holm into a room with lofty but barred windows, bare gleaming walls, devoid of the slightest ornamentation. A few beds were placed along a wall, of which only a single one was occupied. A faint smell of drugs greeted him ; a man in a gaol constable's uniform sat beside the bed, and Holm understood that he had come to a prison hospital.

A small electric lamp was burning from the ceiling, and by its gleam he saw a youthful invalid, with an emaciated face, lying in bed. He had hardly cast a glance at the prisoner before he forgot that he had just been feeling in better humour with George. Now, however, he was ready to spring at him with his old fury.

"What have you to do here ? " he exclaimed. "If you do anything to the man lying in yonder bed we are foes for eternity, so understand that."

The driver turned towards him with a look which was more pitiful than aggressive.

"Now I know who it is who is lying there, David. I did not know till we came here."

"Whether you knew it or not, it is all the same-understand "

He stopped abruptly. George had made a commanding gesture with his hand, and David relapsed into silence, subjugated by an irresistible fear.

"For you and me there is only submission and obedience," the driver warned him. " It is not for you to wish or ask for aught, but only to await quietly for illumination."

With these words George pulled his cowl over his face as a sign that he would not have anything further to say "to him, and, in the silence' which ensued, David Holm observed that the sick prisoner had begun to talk to his warder.

"Do you think, officer, that I shall ever be myself again ? " he asked, in a weak but not at all despondent or melancholy voice.

"Good gracious, Holm, of course you will," said the warder kindly, though in a slightly uncertain tone. " You must pull yourself together a bit, and shake off the fever."

"I take it that you know, officer, that it was not the fever I was thinking about," continued the sick man. " I am wondering if you think I can get out of this prison again ; it's no easy matter when one has been condemned for manslaughter."

" You will do all right, Holm, as you have someone to go to," replied the warder; " at any rate, you said that there was a place where you would be taken in."

An exquisite smile overspread the prisoner's countenance.

"How did the doctor think I was this evening ? " he asked.

" No danger, Holm, no danger. What the doctor said was just this : ' If only I had him outside these walls, I could soon put him on his feet again.' "

The prisoner expanded his chest and sucked in the air between his teeth. " Outside these walls ! " he murmured.

" I am only repeating what the doctor usually says to me," the warder went on ; " but you must not take him too literally and slip away from us, as you did in the autumn of last year. That only means a longer imprisonment, you understand."

"No fear, officer, I am a wiser man now. I'm only thinking of putting an end to this soon, and afterwards beginning a new life."

"Ah ! you're right, it will be a new life," remarked the warder, in a somewhat solemn tone.

Meanwhile David Holm was undergoing worse torture than the sick man.

"They have infected him with his disease in this prison," he mumbled, as he swayed his body to and fro in anguish. " And now he is done for, he who was so handsome, so strong, and so gay."

" Warder," continued the sick man, " have you not " But at that moment he caught a slight movement of impatience in* the warder, and exclaimed: " Perhaps my chattering is against the rules ? "

"No, to-night you may talk, as much as you like."

"To-night! " the sick man repeated thoughtfully. " Ah, yes ! because it!is New Year's Eve? "

" Yes," replied the officer, " because a good New Year is opening for you."

"The fellow sits there, knowing that the poor chap will die to-night," complained the prisoner's brother in his utter helplessness. "That's why he is so gentle with him."

"Have you noticed, officer," and the prisoner took up the question he had broken off short, " that there has been a change in me since I ran away?

You have had no trouble with me since then, have you?"

"You have been like a lamb ever since, so I have had no cause to be annoyed ; but I say, as I said before, don't do it again." "As to that change, officer, have you ever wondered what it was due to ? Perhaps you thought that it was because I became worse in health after the escape ? "

"Well, yes, we all thought something like that."

"But that's not the reason at all," the prisoner -explained; " it comes from something else. I have never dared to speak about it before, but to-night I should like to tell you about it, warder."

"I am afraid, Holm, that you are talking too much," said the warder, but on observing that the man's face grew downcast, he continued in a kindly manner: " Not that I am tired of your talking-it is for your own sake."

"Did not those in the prison think it strange that I came back of my own accord ? " asked the sick man. " Nobody had the least knowledge as to my whereabouts, but I walked into the chief constable's office and gave myself up voluntarily. Why did you think I acted so queerly ? "

"We thought, of course, that you had fared so badly outside that you thought it better to give yourself up of your own accord."

"It is true enough that I did fare badly during the first few days, but I had been away, you know, full three weeks. Did you think I had been out in the wide woods all that time-and in the winter, too?"

"We were bound to believe it, Holm, as you said that it was so."

The prisoner looked amused. "One had sometimes to humbug the authorities in that way, to prevent those who have helped one from getting into trouble. One cannot answer otherwise. Those who have been brave enough to harbour an escaped prisoner, and treat him well, deserve to be helped as much as is in one power. You agree with that; I take it, warder ? "

"Now, Holm, you are asking more than you will get answered," replied the warder, with the same patience that he had shown ail-along.

The young prisoner heaved a deep sigh of longing. " If I could but endure all this, till I reach there again! They were people who lived on the outskirts of the wood."

He broke off and lay fighting for air. The warder looked anxiously at him. He seized hold of a medicine bottle, but, on seeing that it was empty, got up. "I must fetch a little more of this stuff," he said, and left the room.

A moment afterwards the driver took the man's place beside the bed, after putting his scythe where the young man could not see it-then he threw his cowl back.

David Holm burst out wailing like a crying child when he saw that awful figure so near his brother, but the prisoner betrayed no uneasiness. Lying where he did in high fever, he did not observe that a new-comer had seated himself on the chair beside him, but fancied that it was the same warder whom he had continually facing him.

"It was a little cottage," he muttered, panting cruelly after each word.

"Holm, you are not to exert yourself like that with talking," commanded the driver. " The authorities' know every detail of what you are thinking about, but we did not want to betray that we knew."

The sick man opened his eyes wide in astonishment.

"Ah! you are staring at me, Holm," said the driver, " but wait and you shall hear. Do you think that we had no information about a lad who sneaked one afternoon into a little cottage-the last of a row of cottages in a long village-where he thought there would be nobody at home ? He had been lying in hiding, on the outskirts of the wood, till the mistress went out-he assumed that the master would be away at work, and he had not caught sight of any children. When at last the woman went out with a milk-can on her arm, the lad, who had watched where she hid the key, slunk into the cottage."

"How do you know that, warder?" the sick man asked, and in his amazement tried to sit up in bed.

"Just you he still, Holm,"_ replied the driver good-humouredly, " and don't be afraid for your friends. After all, we prison warders are human. Now I'll tell you what I know besides. Well, when that lad entered the cottage, he was frightened because it was not empty, as he had believed it to be. A sick child lay in a big bed against the opposite wall looking at him. He walked softly up to it, but the child closed its eyes and lay as quiet as if it were dead. ' Why are you lying there in the middle of the day ? ' asked the lad. ' Are you ill ?' The child, however, did not stir. ' You mustn't be afraid of me,' said the lad. ' Just tell me where I can as quickly as possible get a little food, and then I'll be off.'

"As the child lay absolutely still and would not answer, the intruder pulled a straw out of the mattress and tickled it under the nose. The child started sneezing, and then the lad laughed. At first the child gazed at him with astonishment, but soon began to laugh too. ' I thought I would pretend to be dead,' said the child. ' I saw that, but what would be the use of it ?" You have heard, I suppose, that if you meet a bear in the woods, and,throw yourself down and pretend to be already dead, the bear goes away to dig a hole to bury you in, and, while he is doing this, you can get away.' The man turned red in the face at these words. ' Oh, indeed, you thought I was going to dig a hole to cram you in ? ' he said. ' That was mere silliness of me,' replied the child, ' for, in any case, I can't run away. I have something the matter .with my hips, and I can't walk.' "

The sick prisoner seemed quite beside himself with astonishment.

"Perhaps you would prefer my not going on with the story ? " the driver remarked.

"Oh, no! I like hearing it. I like being reminded of it I But I can't make out "

"That's not so remarkable, you know, Holm. There was a tramp called George-possibly you have heard speak of him, sometime or other ? He heard the story in one of his wanderings, and passed it on till at last it reached the prison."

A short silence now ensued, but soon the prisoner asked in his weak voice: " What happened' afterwards to that lad, and that child ? "

"Well, it happened that the lad again begged for food. ' I suppose poor people sometimes call at this cottage and ask for food ? ' he said. ' Yes, that certainly is the case,' replied the child. ' And your mother generally gives them something to eat ? ' ' Yes, if she has anything in the house, she gives them something.' ' Well, you see,' said the lad, ' that's just the question now; it's only a poor chap who has come to you to ask for food. Tell me where there is something to eat, and I won't take more than sufficient to satisfy me.' The child gazed at him with a funny precocious look. ' Mother was thinking about this fugitive who is said to be running wild in the woods, so she put all the food away and locked the cupboard.' ' But you saw, didn't you, where she put the key, so you might tell me ? Otherwise I shall be obliged to force open the cupboard.' ' That won't be easy,' said the child; because we have a strong lock to our cupboard.

"The lad went all round the cottage, searching for the; keys. He searched underneath the stove, and in the table-drawer, but could find nothing. Meanwhile the child was sitting up in bed, peeping out of; the window. Here come a lot of people down the road-mother and a whole crowd of others,' he said. The fugitive made a spring and stood by the door. ' If you go out, you will run right into them,' remarked the child. ' It would be better for you to hide in our cupboard.' The lad lingered by the door. ' That is true, but I haven't the cupboard key.' 'Here it is, though,' said the child, stretching out his hand, which held a big key.

"The fugitive took the key and rushed to the cupboard. ' Throw the key here,' shouted the child, after the lad had opened the door; ' you fasten the door from the inside.' He obeyed, and next minute had shut himself in. Likely -enough the lad's heart beat fast when he listened to his pursuers. He heard the door of the outer room open, and then a crowd of people came in. A woman's voice Cried high and shrill: ' Has anybody been here ? ' ' Yes, mother,' said the child ; 'a young man came-in soon after you had gone.' ' Good gracious ! Good gracious !' the woman whimpered. ' It was the one they said that they saw coming from the woods and entering this cottage.'

"The fugitive swore silently to himself at what he thought was the child's treachery. That smart boy had caught him, as it were, in a rat-trap. He began pushing at the door, so as to rush out headlong and, perhaps, contrive to break through. Then he heard someone ask which way the man had gone. ' He is not here now,' said the clear childish voice; 'he was frightened when he saw you coming.'

Has he taken anything ?' asked the mother. ' No, he wanted food, but I had none to give him.' ' But didn't he do anything to you ? ' ,' He tickled me under the nose with a straw,' replied the child, ' and the runaway heard how I laughed.' ' Oh, did he ?' said the mother, who laughed now that her anxiety had been dispelled.

'We are not, I suppose, going to stay gaping at these walls when the fellow is not here,' said a man's voice, and directly afterwards the people could be heard leaving the cottage. 'You will stay at home now, Lisa? ' someone was heard to say. 'Yes, I don't mean to leave Bernard again to-day,' answered the mother.

'The fugitive, on hearing the outer door shut, concluded .that the mother and child were now alone in the room. ' What will be best for me ? ' he thought. ' Shall I remain here or try to make off? ' Just then he heard a step approaching the cupboard. 'Don't be frightened, you who are inside, but come out so that I may have a word with you,' cried the mother. Whereat she put the key into the lock and opened the door. The lad stepped timidly put. 'It was the kid who told me that T could hide here,' he said, pointing to the child.

"The little boy was so excited by the adventure that he clapped his hands in glee. ' That small chap of mine gets so shrewd by always lying still and thinking his own thoughts,' said the mother proudly. ' Soon nobody will be sharp enough for him.' The fugitive' understood that she was not going to surrender him to the police, because the boy had taken a fancy to him. ' You are right there,' he replied. ' I may tell you that I walked in here to get myself a little food, but I could not light on any. This boy would not give me the key. He's cleverer than many a one who can walk on his feet.' The mother, no doubt, saw what his drift was by his flattery, but, all the same, she liked hearing it. 'I will give you something to eat first of all,' she said. While the fugitive was eating, the boy began asking particulars of his escape, and the man told his story truthfully from beginning to end. His flight had not been premeditated, but he happened to find an opportunity on an occasion when he had work in the prisonyard-the gates had been thrown open to admit a load of hay being carried through. The boy questioned and questioned him insatiably as to how he had contrived to get clear of the town and reach the woods. Twice the lad said that he really ought to stop, but the boy would not hear of it. ' You are quite welcome to sit here to-night and chat with Bernard,' said the mother at last. ' There's such a lot of people on the look-out ior you that, likely enough, you will be taken whether you stay here or steal away.'

"The fugitive was still relating his adventures when the master of the house arrived. It was dark in the room, and the cottager thought at first that it was one" of the neighbours sitting chatting with the child. 'Is that you, Petter, telling Bernard fairy tales ? ' he asked. The child began laughing again in his excitement. ' No, father, it isn't Petter; it's someone much better. Come here and you shall hear.' The father went to the bed, but he learnt nothing till he put his ears to the child's lips. ' It's the man who escaped ! ' whispered the boy. ' Good gracious, Bernard, what things you do say ! ' cried the father. ' Well, it's true,' said the child. ' He has been telling me how he stole out of the prison gates and lay for three whole nights in an old lumber-shed in the woods. I know all about it! '

"The mother had hurriedly lighted a small lamp, and the peasant now looked at the fugitive, who had taken his stand by the door. ' I must hear how that tale hangs together,' said the cottager. So they began the story, wife and child both talking, and both equally excited. The peasant was an oldish man, and he looked wise and thoughtful. He eyed the runaway prisoner narrowly, whilst the others were chattering. ' He looks, to say the least of it, mortally ill, poor fellow ! ' he thought. ' If he sleeps another night in that lumber-shed, it will certainly be all up with him.'

" ' There are many people walking the streets, whom no one thinks of arresting, but who look more dangerous customers than you,' he said, when the others were silent. ' I am not really dangerous,' . said the fugitive ; ' it was someone who roused my temper when I was drunk!' The peasant would not let him say anything further on the matter, " lest the boy should hear it. 'I can imagine that it happened that way,' he said, interrupting.

"It was quite silent hi the room now ; the peasant sat immersed in thought, the others watching him anxiously. Nobody dared say another word to influence him in favour of the lad. At last he turned towards his wife. ' I don't know if I am doing wrong, but it is the same with me as with you-since the boy has taken a fancy to him, I can't drive him away.'

"It was therefore agreed that the fugitive should stay the night and leave early next morning. Before long, however, he developed so bad an attack of fever that he could not stand on his legs, so, because of that, they had to keep him in the cottage for a fortnight."

It was curious to watch the two brothers who were listening to this story, when the driver got to the point where the fugitive was staying with the peasants. The sick lad had stretched himself on his bed, and was lying at perfect ease. His pains seemed to have left him, and he was brooding over happy bygones. The other was still suspicious, surmising that behind all this some trap was hidden. He. tried again and again to make a sign to his brother not to be so confident, but he could not catch the latter's eye.

"They dared not send for a doctor," said the driver, going on with his story, "nor could they venture to the chemist's for physic. The sick lad had to get well without all that. If anybody called and seemed about to enter the cottage, the mistress went to the entrance and said that Bernard had such a suspicious looking rash on his body — she was afraid it might be scarlet fever-that she could not take the responsibility of admitting anyone.

"About a fortnight afterwards, when the fugitive began to rally, he said to himself that it would not do for him to stay longer with his host and hostess-he must wander farther on. He could not continue to be a burden to these poor people.

"About that time they began speaking to him on a subject that weighed on him heavily. It so happened that Bernard asked him one evening where he was going after he left them. 'I suppose I shall take to the woods again,' he answered. ' But it will be precious little good your going out into the wilds,' said the peasant's wife. ' If I were you, I should make a clean breast of it to the police authorities. There cannot really be much pleasure in roaming about like a wild animal.' ' Nor is there any pleasure in being in gaol! ' ' No, yet when the thing has to be done, it is always better to get it done sooner, than later.' 'My sentence' had nearly expired,' the lad said, ' but now I shall probably have it increased.' ' Yes, it was a mistake, your running away,' said the wife. ' No ! ' answered the lad briskly; ' it was the best thing I did in all my life.'

"In saying this, he looked at the boy and smiled, and the child nodded to him and laughed. He loved that youngster-he would have liked to lift him out of bed and carry him away on his shoulders when he quitted the cottage. ' It will be very difficult for you to meet Bernard again if you continue wandering about all your life as a poor runaway ! ' 'It will be a sight worse if I let them clap me into prison.'

"The peasant sat by the fire and now joined in the conversation. ' We were beginning to get on well together,' he said, in his grave way, ' but we can't hide you any longer from the neighbours, now that you are able to get about. It would be quite another matter if you had been discharged from prison.' The fugitive felt a sudden suspicion —they would perhaps make him give himself up, in order to avoid future trouble with the authorities ! So he answered : ' I am so well now that I can go my way to-morrow morning.' ' That wasn't what I meant,' said the peasant, ' but if you had been free, I should have invited you to stay on with us and help in the farming.'

"The fugitive, who was well aware how hard it was for.a convict to find a situation, was touched by this offer, but there was much against his returning to prison, and he sat silent.

"That evening the boy was worse than usual. ' Ought he not to be sent to the hospital for treatment?' asked the fugitive. 'He has been there several times, but they say that nothing will do him any good except sea-bathing. How can we afford that ? ' 'It would be a long journey, I suppose ? ' said the visitor. ' It's not the journey, but he would need money'for bed and board.' ' Ah ! then, of course, it is impossible.' "There was silence for a long while, but the fugitive played with the thought that, perhaps, some day'he might be able to get Bernard the money for the journey.

"He turned to the peasant and took up the subject they had been discussing. ' It is none so easy to take a convict into one's service,' he said tentatively. ' It would work all right, I think,' replied the peasant, ' but possibly you are one of' those who don't feel comfortable in the country but must needs live in a town." I never think.of town life,' remarked the convict, ' when I am sitting in my cell. I think of nothing but the woods and the fields.'

"'When you have completed your sentence, you will feel as though much that now weighs on your mind will be gone,' said the peasant. ' Yes, that's just what I say too,' chimed in the wife.

" 'If you could sing to us, Bernard-but perhaps you are too ill for that.' ' Oh, no !' said the child. ' I rather think your friend would like it,' the mother suggested. The convict felt nervous, as if fearing a misfortune. He wanted to ask the boy not to sing, but the latter had already begun. He sang in a clear, gentle voice, and he never worried so much about his being a prisoner for life, yearning for freedom and movement, when he sang.

"The convict hid his face in his hands, but the tears dropped through his fingers. ' I myself can never be anything worthy,' he thought; ' but I must do something to give that child his freedom.'

"Next day he bade the family farewell. Nobody asked him where he was going-all they said was: ' Welcome here again ! ' ' "

Yes, so they did, warder," remarked the sick man, at last interrupting the driver. " That, mark you, is the one and only beautiful incident in my ^whole fife." He lay silent, but two tears softly coursed down his cheeks. "lam glad that you know all this, warder," he went on. " Now I can -tell you about Bernard. I think that I have been liberated —I think that I have been with him. I couldn't have believed that I should be so happy to-night "

"Listen to me, Holm," the driver interrupted. " If I could so arrange it that you might visit your friends now and at once, but in a different way than you ever dreamt of, what would you say ? If I invited you to escape the long years of longing and gave you your freedom this very night, would you be willing ? "

Whilst uttering these words, the driver threw back his cowl and grasped the scythe.

The sick lad looked at him with big eyes that were filled with longing.

"Do you understand what I mean, Holm?" asked the driver. " Understand that I am he who can open all prisons; I am he who can carry you to a height beyond the reach of any pursuers ?"

"I understand what you mean,'" the prisoner whispered, " but would not that be doing Bernard a wrong ? You know that I came back here so that I might gain my liberty in an honourable manner-in order that I might help him."

"You made for him the highest sacrifice in your power, and, in reward for that„ your punishment has been shortened, and the freedom that is beyond all price is offered to you. You need not think of him any more."

"Oh, but I should have taken him to the seaside," replied the lad. " I whispered to him When we parted that I would come back and take him to the sea. One ought to keep one's promise to a child ! "

"So you don't care to accept the freedom that I am offering you ? " said the driver, getting up.

"Oh, yes ; oh, yes !" cried the lad, laying hold of his garment. "Don't go. You know not what my longing is. If only there was another who might help him but he has no one except myself."

The sick'lad looked wearily round his cell.

"My brother David is sitting over there," he cried, " so it is all right. I can ask him to help Bernard."

"Your brother David!" repeated the driver. " No, you can't ask him to take care of a child. You should see how he treats his own."

"David," the prisoner entreated, " I see before me green lawns and the free, open sea. You understand, David —I have been a prisoner here so long! I cannot accept, when I am invited to fly away to freedom, without committing a wrong by so doing. I must not break faith with that child. You know, I made a promise."

"Don't be uneasy, lad," replied David Holm, in a trembling voice. " As to that child, and those people who helped you, I promise you that I will help them. Go! take your freedom-go where you will. I will look after them. Walk calmly out of your prison ! "

At these words thesick man fell suddenly back on his pillow.

' You spoke to him, David, the words of death ! Let us hence; it is time for us to be gone. The freed soul must not be met by us who live in captivity and darkness ! "

" Were it possible to make oneself heard in this horrible creaking and rattling," thought David Holm, " I should like, to say a few words of thanks to George for having helped those two-Sister Edith and my brother-in their last moments. I won't satisfy him by releasing him from his office, but I should very much like to show him that I appreciate the way in which he came to their assistance."

Hardly had these thoughts crossed his mind before the driver pulled the reins and stopped the horse, just as if he had anticipated these thoughts.

" I am only a poor bungler of a carter," he remarked, " but sometimes I have the luck to help someone-though it happens quite as often that I fail. These two were easy to carry over the boundary, because the one longed so ardently for God's heaven, and the other had so little to bind him to earth. Know this, David," he went on, assuming the old friendly tone, " that many a time when sitting listening in this cart, I have thought to myself that if I could but send a certain message to mankind, what I should send them would certainly be a.greeting."

"I can well imagine that to be so," said David Holm.

"You know, David, that it is no sorrow to be a reaper when the field stands full of ripened grain ; but if one is forced to mow down poor and only half-grown plants, he might think that a cruel and thankless work. ' The husbandman whom I serve regards Himself as too good for such, and leaves it all for me, a poor carter."

"I understood that it had to be so," remarked David Holm.

"If men but knew," continued George, " how easy it is to help across the boundary those who have their work ready, and their duties fulfilled, and the bonds almost broken, and how hard it is to free him who has attempted nothing, accomplished nothing,, and leaves behind him all he loves, then perhaps they would try to make the driver's task a less irksome one."

"What do you mean, George ? "

"Think of one thing, David. All the time you have been with me, you have hardly heard any talk of more than one disease. I can assure you that was the same with me all the years. It is because the disease spreads among the unripe seeds that it falls to my lot to reap. During the first period of my driving the death-cart, I was always thinking that if only that disease were — removed, my office would be Considerably lightened."

"Was that the greeting you wanted to send to mankind ? "

"No, David. I know better now than I did then what man can do. Some day. the.y certainly ought to vanquish this enemy with the weapons of science and perseverance. They should never rest till they have freed themselves from that, and all other great diseases which, strike them down, before their maturity. The matter does not depend on this."

"How should they, then, lighten the driver's work?"

"Men are so eager to arrange everything for the best for themselves in their world," replied George, " that I think the day will come when poverty and drunkenness and all such wretchedness that shortens life will no longer exist, but that does not imply that the driver's occupation will be less toilsome."

"What greeting, then, would you send them, George? "

"It will soon be New Year's morning, David, and when men awake their first thoughts will be upon the New Year and all that they wish and hope . that it may give them-after that, on their future. But the greeting I would send them is not that they should wish for luck in love-affairs, success, or power, or a long, or even a healthy life. I would have them fold their hands and concentrate their thoughts upon a single prayer:

" ' O God! vouchsafe that my soul may come to maturity ere it shah be reaped ! ' "

CHAPTER VIII
DAVID HOLM RETURNS TO PRISON

Two women were sitting engrossed in a conversation which had lasted many hours. It had been interrupted for a time in the afternoon, when the pair had been engaged in. holding divine service in the Salvationists' quarters, but, at its close, the conversation had been resumed. During the whole of the time one of the women had been trying Very hard to infuse courage and confidence into the other, but it appeared to have been labour in vain.

"Understand, Mrs. Holm," said she who was trying to console and cheer the other, " that, strange as it may sound, I believe there is a better time in store for you. I believe that David has now done his worst. That was, I take it, something he.had set himself to do, in order to slake the vengeance he has threatened you with ever since you came to be reunited. But, Mrs. Holm, it is one thing for Mm to be cruel one day and say that his children are not to be taken away, and another thing for him to cherish in his heart such a murderous thought and carry it out day after day. I don't believe that anyone could persist in such a course."

"Captain, you are very good to try to console me," replied the wife, though it was evident that she thought in her heart that if the Salvationist Captain did not know anyone capable of a thing like that, she herself certainly knew one who was.

The Captain looked as if she had now reached the limit of her power to convince, but, all of a sudden, she determined to make a fresh effort.

"You are to bear in mind one thing, Mrs. Holm. I don't say that it was a great sin you committed when you ran away from your husband some years back, but I regard it as a neglect of duty. You left him to his own devices, and it was not long, either, before the evil consequences became evident. For years, however, you have tried to make reparation for it. Now you have acted as- it is God's will that we should act, and I think that there must be a change for the better. It was a big storm that was raised then, and one not to be quelled in an instant, but the work that you and Sister Edith began is one of the good sort, and will bear the fruits of all good works."

When the Captain was saying this, she was no longer alone in the room with Mrs. Holm, for David himself and his friend George-or, more precisely put, their spectres-had found their way into the. room while she was talking, and had taken up their stand by the door.

David Holm was no longer bound hand and foot; he followed the driver without coercion; but when he observed where he had been carried, a sudden resentment arose within him. Here surely no one was about to die ! Why then compel him to see his wife and children again ? He was about to turn to George with an angry question, when the latter made signs to him to keep quiet.

David Holm's wife lifted up her head as if cheered by the other's strong conviction. "If, after all, one could believe that . it was true I " she sighed.

"It is true," persisted the Salvationist, smiling at her. " To-morrow there will be a change. You will see that help will come to you with the New Year."

"The New Year I " repeated the wife. " Yes, it is New Year's Eve —I had forgotten it altogether. How late can it be, Captain Ahdersson ? "

"We are well into the New Year already," came the reply, and she glanced at her watch. "It is a quarter to two."

"Then you must not sit any longer with me, Captain, but go home to bed. I am quite calm now, you see."

The Salvationist Captain gave the woman a searching look.

"There's something, though, that seems to me not altogether satisfactory about that calmness of yours."

"You need have no apprehension about me, Captain," replied the wife. " I know that I have said some hard things to-night, but it is over now."

"Do you mean, Mrs. Holm, that you can put everything into God's Hands and trust to Him to arrange everything for the best?" asked the Captain.

"Yes," the wife assured her, " I can."

"I would willingly have stayed till the morning, but I see that .you think it better that I should go."

"It has been so nice to have you here, but David will soon be coming now, so I ought to be by myself."

They both went out of the room after interchanging a few more words. David Holm knew that his wife was accompanying the Salvationist Captain to the door to open it for her.

"David," said the driver, " did you hear her? You observe that human beings know all they need to know ? They have only to be strengthened in the desire, to will to live long and well."

He had scarcely said this before the wife returned. It was obvious that she meant to keep her promise and go to bed. She sat on a chair and began unlacing a boot.

While she was doing this, the house door slammed noisily. The woman at once got up and listened. " Is he coming ? " she wondered. " Surely it is David coming."

She rushed to the window and tried to look down to the dark yard. She stood thus for a couple of minutes, scrutinising it intently. When she returned to the chair, her face had strangely altered. It had become grey-eyes, lips, all of her-as if covered with ashes; her movements were stiff and stumbling, and a slight twitching passed over her lips.

"I can't endure it! " she whispered, "I can't endure it! "

"Yes, I will trust in God! " she cried, a few moments later, standing in the middle of the room. " They tell me that I must trust in God-they think that, perhaps, I have not prayed to Him and called on Him. What shall I do ? How shall I contrive to get any help from Him ? "

She was not weeping, but her speech was a prolonged moan. She was under the sway of a despair so great that she was evidently not responsible for her actions.

David Holm leant forward, eyed her sharply, and started at a sudden thought.

The wife did not walk, but stumbled towards the bed in the corner, where her two children were lying asleep.

"It is a pity," she murmured, bending over them, " that they are so pretty."

She knelt on the floor beside them, gazing for a while first on one and then on the other.

"But I must get away," she said, " and I can't leave them behind me."

She stroked their heads awkwardly and as if unused to it.

"You must not be angry with me for what I am doing," she continued, "for it is not my fault."

While she was kneeling on the floor, caressing the children, the outer door banged again. The woman jumped up again and was obviously nervous till she realised that it was not her husband who had come in. " I must make haste," she said to the children, in a weird whisper. " It shall be done quickly, provided David does not come and prevent me.

However, she did nothing at the moment except pace up and down the room.

"There is something that tells me to wait till the morning," she murmured, half-aloud, "but what good will that be ? To-morrow will be a day like all the rest. Why should he be kinder to-morrow than to-day ? "

David Holm was thinking about that corpse which was lying in the shrubbery, and which would soon be buried in the earth as useless for anything else. He was longing for his wife to know in some way that she need no longer be afraid of him.

Again a slight noise was heard. It was a door in the house being opened and shut, and again the wife trembled as she remembered the purpose she had in mind. She slipped to the stove and began putting in some wood, so as to kindle a fire.

"It does not matter if he does come and sees me making a fire," she said aloud, in reply to some silent objection. " I may, I suppose, boil some coffee on New Year's morning, so as to have something to keep me awake while waiting up for him."

David Holm felt a great relief when she said this. Again he began to wonder what purpose George had in mind when bringing him here. Nobody was about to die-nobody was ill.

The driver stood motionless, with his cowl drawn down, and so preoccupied was he that it would not do to question him.

"He wants me to see my wife and family for the last time," David decided. " I shall never be in; their presence again. That does not make me a whit unhappy," he continued, a moment later, thinking that he had ho room in his heart save for one; but he went to the corner where the two children were lying. Whilst standing there, he began to think about the little boy whom his brother loved so much that, for his sake, he even returned to prison of his own accord-he felt, with a sense of inferiority, that he did not love his children like that.

"May it, in any case, go well for them in this world I" he thought with sudden tenderness. .. " They will rejoice to-morrow when they hear that they need not be afraid of their father any longer.

"I wonder what sort of creatures they will turn out, when they are grown up," he wondered, with a more lively interest than he had ever before displayed over them, and he felt at the same time a sudden fear lest they should be such as he himself. " I've been an exceedingly unhappy man. I don't understand why I did not trouble myself about them before. If there is any return for me, I will come back and make real men of these two."

He paused and examined the state of his heart. "It is curious that I no longer feel any hatred towards my wife," he murmured. " I should like her to be happy, after all that she has suffered.' Were it possible, I would get back all that furniture for her, and I should like to see her go to church on Sundays in nice clothes. But she will, of course, get all that and more, now that I am out of her path. I believe that George has brought me here so that I may be glad to be among the dead ! "

At that moment he gave a sudden start. He had been so engrossed in his thoughts as to pay no attention to what his wife was about. Now, however, he uttered a cry of anguish.

" It's boiling-the water's boiling; it will soon be ready. It must be done at once, for there is no time to lose."

The woman took down a pot that was standing on a shelf close to the stove, and poured from it some ground coffee into the vessel. This done, she took from her bosom a little packet containing a white powder, which she also put in the water.

David Holm stood staring at her, without daring to put into thought the meaning of what she was doing.

"You shall see, David, that this will do it!" she said aloud, turning towards the room just as if she saw him. " That will suffice for both children and myself. I can't stand any longer seeing the children pining away. If you only stop out another hour or so, everything will be done as you wanted by the time you return."

Now the man could not remain any longer listening quietly ; he hurried to the driver.

"George ! " he" cried. " Oh, good God ! don't you understand what is going on ? "

"Yes, David, I do," replied the driver, "I am standing here —I am obliged to be present. I can't evade my duty ! "

"But surely, George, you don't understand; it's not only my wife, but also the children. She means to take them with her ! "

"Yes, David," the driver admitted, " she means to take your children with her."

"But that must not be! It is unnecessary, you know. Can't you make her realise that it is unnecessary?"

"I cannot make myself heard by her-she is too far away."

"But can't you summon someone here, George-someone who will tell her that it is no longer necessary? "

"You are asking absurdities, David. What power have I over the living ? "

David Holm refused to be deterred from his purpose. He threw himself on his knees before the driver.

" Remember that you were once my friend and companion, and do not suffer this thing to be done! Let not this befall me-do not suffer the poor innocent children to die."

He looked up at George for an answer, but the latter only shook his head in refusal:

"I will do all in my power for you, George. I refused when you told me to take, your place as driver, but I gladly accept that service, provided that I escape going through this awful trial. They are so tiny, both of them-and just now I was wishing that I could have lived to make good men of them. And she-she is insane to-night; she does not know what she is doing! Have pity on her, George!"

When the driver remained motionless, he turned a little aside from him.

"I am so lonely, so lonely! " he cried. " I do not know where to turn. I do not even, know whether to pray to God or to Christ. I am a newcomer in this world. Who is it that has the power ? Who can tell me to Whom I can betake myself in prayer?

"Oh, I, a poor sinful man, pray to Him who is Lord of life and of death. I am not fit to stand forth and pray. I have,, in good sooth, wrought against all Thy laws and ordinances, but suffer me to go into the uttermost darkness. Let nothing remain of me: Do what Thou wilt with me, so that these three innocents be spared."

David held his peace and listened for an answer, but all he heard was his wife talking to herself.

"Now that this is melted and boiled, it will only have to stand and cool for a few moments."

Then George bent down to his companion, his cowl thrown back and his face brightened with a smile. " David," he said, "if you are really in earnest, there is perhaps still a means of saving them. You yourself must let your wife know that she need not be afraid of you."

"But I cannot make myself heard by. her, can I, George ? "

"No, not as you are. You must return to the David Holm who is lying in the shrubbery. Can you do that ? "

David shuddered with fright. Human life seemed to him something suffocating and deadly. Would not the soul's fresh development stop, if he became a mortal once more ? All his happiness was awaiting, him in another world !

Nevertheless, he did not hestitate a second.

"If I can-if I am free. I thought that I should have to. "

" Yes, you are right," replied George, and his countenance gleamed with still greater beauty. " You must be Death's driver for the whole of this year, unless another undertakes to perform the office in your stead."

"Another ? " exclaimed David Holm. " Who would sacrifice himself for a wretch like me? "

"David, there is a man who.has never ceased to bewail that he seduced you from the path of virtue. Perhaps that man would perform your office gladly, because he need never again have to grieve for you.

Without giving David time to understand fully the purport of his words, he bent over him, gazing with radiant eyes on his face.

Old friend, David Holm, do the best you can. I shall remain here till you return. You have not a long time left."

"But you, George "

The driver checked him by that commanding gesture of the hand which he had learnt to obey. In a flash, he threw back his cowl, and cried in a loud and ringing voice :

"Prisoner, return to your prison! "

David Holm leant on his elbow and looked round about him. All the street lamps were extinguished, but it had grown light, and the half-moon was shining. He had no difficulty in assuring himself, that he was still lying in the church shrubbery, on the withered grass-plot overshadowed by the dark branches of the lime-trees.

Without a moment's reflection, he began getting to his feet. He felt absolutely weary; bis body was stiff with cold and his head swam; but he managed somehow to raise himself up from the grass, after which he began stumbling in the direction of the avenue. So near was he to falling, that he was obliged to steady himself against a tree.

"I am not up to it," he thought. " It will be impossible for me to be there in time."

Not for an instant did he feel that what he had gone through was an illusion-he had the fullest and most definite impressions left of the night's events.

"I left the driver waiting in my house," he muttered he. "I needs must hasten." "He left the tree that he had been leaning against, and took several steps forward, but he was so pitifully weak that he sank to his knees.

Then, in this terrible moment of abandonment, he felt something brush against his forehead. He did not know whether it was a hand, or a pair of lips-or, possibly, the flapping of very thin garments —but it was enough to ravish his whole soul with bliss.

" She has returned to me I " he cried in jubilation ; "she is near me again; she is protecting me."

He stretched out his hands in ecstasy at being encompassed by the beloved's, love, at her love filling, his heart with gladness even at the moment when he-had returned to the earthly sphere.

He heard footsteps behind him in the deserted night. A small woman, whose head was covered by a big Salvationist bonnet, came tripping by.

" Sister Mary! " he cried, as she was going past him. "Sister Mary, help me!" The Slum-Sister may have recognised the voice.

She shrank away and pursued her course without troubling about him. '

" Sister Mary, I am not drunk. I am ill! Help me to get home."

Well, she scarcely believed him, but, without another word, she went to him, helped him to rise, and supported him as he walked.

He was once more on his way home, but how slow was the journey. All might be over by now! The man stopped suddenly.

"Sister Mary, it would be a great boon if you would go to my home first, and fell the wife -"

"Need I tell her that you are coming back, drunk as usual ? Is she so unused to it ? "

David bit his lips and struggled on, striving to the uttermost to increase his pace; but his body, half-paralysed by cold, refused obedience.

Soon he made another effort to induce her to hurry forward in advance of him. "I have been asleep and dreaming," he said. " I have seen Sister Edith die —I saw Sister Edith on her death-bed; I have also seen my wife and children at home. She is not in her right mind to-night. I tell you, Sister Mary, if you don't hurry on before me she will do herself a mischief."

His words came weak and broken. The Sister made no answer, as she persisted in her opinion that she had a drunkard to deal with. 'Nevertheless she helped him on. He realised that she had won a hard-fought victory over herself in consenting to aid one whom she regarded as mainly instrumental in causing Sister Edith's death.

Whilst David Holm was stumbling along, he became the prey to a fresh anxiety. How was he to get himself believed by the poor woman at home, who was so frightened of him, unless Sister Mary

At last they stood before the gate of the yard in which he lived, and the Sister helped him to open it.

"Now you can, I suppose, look after yourself," she said, preparing to go.

"It would be very kind indeed, Sister Mary, if you would shout to my wife to come and assist me."

The woman shrugged her shoulders. " Understand, David Holm, on another night I might perhaps have looked better after you, but to-night I have not the heart to do it. This, must suffice for the present."

Her voice died away in a burst of sobs, and she hurried away from him.

As Holm made his way with difficulty up the steep flight of stairs, it seemed to him that it must be too late-and, in any case, how could he make his wife believe in him?

Whilst he was almost sinking on the stairs from weariness and despondency, he again felt that- soft caress on his brow.

"She is near me ; she is watching over me ! " and he found strength at last to toil up to the top floor.

When he opened the door, his wife stood right in front of him-as if she had hurried to bolt the door to prevent him coming in. On finding that she was too late, she withdrew to the stove and stood with her back to it, as though she had something there she wanted to hide and preserve.

"She has not done it! I have come in time !"

With a rapid glance at the children, he- assured himself that that was actually the case. " They are still asleep. She has not done it I I have come in the nick of time," he said to himself.

He extended his hand to the side where the Death-cart driver, George, had stood but a short time back. He fancied that another hand clasped and pressed it. " Thanks I " he whispered softly, and his voice trembled, a sudden mist came over his eyes.

He stumbled into the room and sank down into a chair. He saw that his wife was watching his movements, just as she would have done if a wild beast had entered the room.

"She really believes that I am drunk-she too ! " he thought.

A new feeling of hopelessness came over him, because he was so unutterably weary and could not get rest. A bed stood in the inner room, and he longed to stretch his limbs on it and not have to hold himself erect; but he dared not go there-his wife would carry out her fell purpose directly he turned his back. He must stay up and watch her.

"Sister Edith is dead," he managed to say, " and I was with her. I promised her that I would be good to you and to the children. You must send them to the home to-morrow."

"Why are you lying ? " his wife demanded. "Gustawson was here, and spoke to Captain Andersson about Sister Edith being dead. He said that you had not gone to her."

David Holm sank on to a chair, and, to his own great astonishment, he began to weep. It was fruitless his returning to the world of thoughts, to the world of closed eyes, which weighed him down. It was a paralysing conviction that he would never get outside the wall which his own ill-deeds had erected round him, a yearning — a boundless yearning-to fuse himself with the soul which hovered over him, a soul, however, which was beyond his reach, which occasioned his tears.

Whilst the heavy weeping was shaking him, he heard his wife's voice.

"David is weeping! " she said to herself, in a tone of indescribable astonishment; and again, about a minute afterwards, she repeated the words : " He is weeping ! "

She left the stove and approached him with evident anxiety.

"Why are you weeping, David ? " she asked.

He lifted up to her a face which was bedewed with tears.

"I will reform," he said with clenched teeth, in a way which might almost have given the impression of his being angry. "I mean to become a really good man. But nobody will believe me. Should I not weep then ? "

" You see, David, it is so hard to believe it," his wife replied dubiously; but I do believe you, now that you are weeping. I do believe you now."

To give him a proof that she felt a renewed trust in him she sat at his feet and leant her head against his knees. She sat perfectly still for a while, but she, too, soon began to weep.

David started. " What ! you weeping also?" ."I cannot help it ! I can't be happy until I have wept away all the sorrow that lies in me.

At that moment David again felt that wonderful cold puff on his brow. His tears ceased, and in their place came a mysterious inward smile from the depths of his soul.

He had fulfilled the first duty imposed on him by the events of the night ; it now remained to him to succour the boy whom his brother had loved. He must show such people as Sister Mary that Sister Edith was not wrong in bestowing on him her love ; he had to raise his own home from its ruins, he must carry to. mankind the driver's greeting. Then, when all this was done, he would go to the beloved, to the object of his yearnings.

David sat on, feeling exceedingly old. He had become patient and submissive, as the old are wont to be; he dared riot either hope, or wish.

He clasped his hands and whispered the Driver's prayer:

" O God ! vouchsafe that my soul may come TO MATURITY ERE IT BE REAPED !